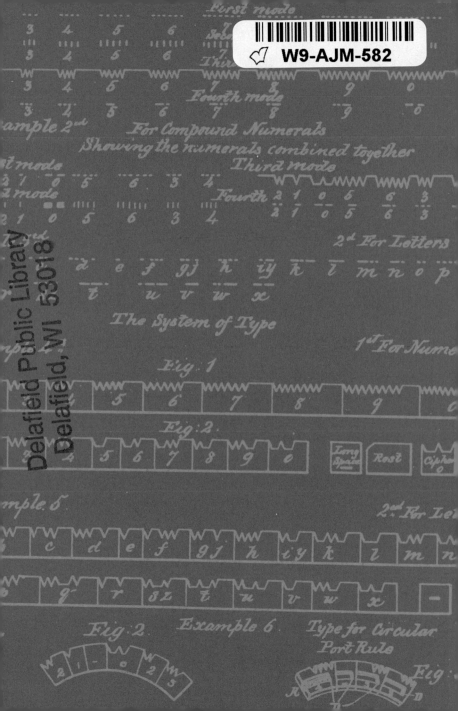

SWIFT AS DESIRE

SWIFT AS DESIRE

A NOVEL

LAURA ESQUIVEL

TRANSLATED BY STEPHEN LYTLE

CROWN PUBLISHERS

NEW YORK

Copyright © 2001 by Laura Esquivel

Translation copyright © 2001 by Stephen A. Lytle

Grateful acknowledgment is made to Peer Music for lyrics from "Pobre De Mi" by Agustin Lara. Copyright © 1941 by Promotora Hispano Americana de Musica, S.A. Administered by Peer International Corporation. Copyright renewed. International copyright secured. Used by permission. All rights reserved.

Published by Crown Publishers, New York, New York.
Member of the Crown Publishing Group.

Random House, Inc. New York, Toronto, London, Sydney, Auckland
www.randomhouse.com

CROWN is a trademark and the Crown colophon is a registered trademark of Random House, Inc.

Printed in the United States of America

Design by Lauren Dong

Library of Congress Cataloging-in-Publication Data

Esquivel, Laura
    [Tan veloz como el deseo. English]
    Swift as desire / Laura Esquivel. — 1st ed.
       p.   cm.
    I. Title.

  PQ_7298.15.S638 T3613 2001
  863'.64—dc21   2001028351

ISBN 0-609-60870-3

10 9 8 7 6 5 4 3 2 1

First Edition

Endpapers: Madrid Codex, courtesy Government Information Resources, Central University Libraries, Southern Methodist University; Morse code chart (Chart Depicting Morse Code Signs, 1840) copyright: Bettmann/CORBIS

In memory of my father, Julio Cesar Esquivel

SWIFT AS DESIRE

INTRODUCTION

YOU CAN FEEL THE NORTH. It takes hold of you, marks you. No matter how far you move from its center of gravity, you are invariably drawn to it by an invisible current, like water droplets to the earth, like a needle to a magnet, like blood to blood, desire to desire.

My origins are in the north, in the first look of love between my grandparents, in the first brush of their hands. The project I would later become was begun with the birth of my mother. I had only to wait for her desire to be united with my father's for me to be drawn irrevocably into this world.

At what precise moment did the powerful, magnetic gaze of the north meet that of the sea? Because the other half of my origin comes from the sea, from the origin of my origin. My father was born near the sea. There, before the green waves, my grandparents' desires became one: to give him a place in this world.

How long did it take for desire to send the right signal, and for the anticipated response to arrive? There were many variables, but it is undeniable that the entire process began with a look. A look which led the way, a suggestive path that the lovers would walk upon later, again and again. Could I have witnessed that first look exchanged between my parents? Where was I when it happened?

I can't stop thinking of all this now as I notice the lost look on my father's face, as his mind wanders, unconscious, through space. Could he be looking for other universes? Fresh desires? New looks, to entice him into another world? I have no way of knowing. He can no longer speak.

I would like to know what he hears, what call he awaits. To know who will draw him into the next world and when. What will the departure signal be? Who will give it? Who will guide him? If women are the doors to life in this world, are we in the next? What midwife will come to his aid?

I like to believe that the incense I keep burning in my father's room is creating a link, a life, a cord by which he will receive the help he needs. The billowing columns of mysterious, heavily scented smoke continuously rise up into the air in spirals, and I can't stop thinking that they are forming an umbilical cord that will connect my father with the celestial strata to take him back to the place from which he came. What I don't know is where that was. And who, or what, is waiting for him out there?

The word *mystery* scares me. To counteract it I cling to memories, to what I know about my *papá*. I imagine that he too is fearful, since his blind eyes cannot discern what is waiting for him.

Since everything begins with a look, I worry that my father won't be able to distinguish other presences, that he won't want to take the first step down another path. How I wish that he will soon be able to see! How I wish for his suffering to end! How I wish for some desire to draw him forward!

"Dear *papi*, you don't know what I would give to be able to light your way. To help you on this journey, just as you helped me with my arrival into this world, do you remember? If I had known that your tender embrace would sustain me so, I wouldn't have waited so long to be born. But how was I to know? Before seeing you and my mother, everything was dark and confusing. Perhaps similar to how your future seems now. But don't worry, I'm sure that wherever you are going, someone is waiting for you, just as you waited for me. I have no doubt that there are eyes that are longing to see you. So go in peace. You are leaving only good memories here. Let these words accompany you. Let the voices of all those who knew you resound in the space around you. Let them open the way for you. Let them be the speakers, the mediators, those who communicate for you. Let them announce the arrival of the loving father, the telegraph operator, the storyteller, the man with the smiling face."

Chapter 1

H E WAS BORN HAPPY and on a holiday. Welcomed into the world by his whole family, gathered together for the special day. They say his mother laughed so hard at one of the jokes being told around the table that her waters broke. At first she thought the dampness between her legs was urine that she had not been able to contain because of her laughter but she soon realized that this was not the case, that the torrent was a signal that her twelfth child was about to be born. Still laughing, she excused herself and went to her bedroom. As she had gone through eleven previous deliveries, this one took only a few minutes, and she gave birth to a beautiful boy who, instead of coming into the world crying, entered it laughing.

After bathing, doña Jesusa returned to the dining room. "Look what happened to me!" she announced to her relatives. Everyone turned to look at her, and, revealing the tiny bundle she held in her arms, she said, "I laughed so hard, the baby came out."

A loud burst of laughter filled the dining room

and everyone enthusiastically applauded the happy occasion. Her husband, Librado Chi, raised his arms and exclaimed, *"¡Qué júbilo!"*—"What joy!"

And that was what they named him. In truth, they could not have chosen a better name. Júbilo was a worthy representative of joy, of pleasure, of joviality. Even when he became blind, many years later, he always retained his sense of humor. It seemed as if he had been born with a special gift for happiness. And I don't mean simply a capacity for being happy, but also a talent for bringing happiness to everyone around him. Wherever he went, he was accompanied by a chorus of laughter. No matter how heavy the atmosphere, his arrival, as if by magic, would always ease tension, calm moods, and cause the most pessimistic person to see the brighter side of life, as if, above all else, he had the gift of bringing peace. The only person with whom this gift failed him was his wife, but that isolated case constituted the sole exception to the rule. In general, there was no one who could resist his charm and good humor. Even Itzel Ay, his paternal grandmother—the woman who, after her son had married a white woman, had been left with a permanent frown etched on her forehead—began to smile when she saw Júbilo. She called him Che'ehunche'eh Wich, which in the Mayan language means "the one with the smiling face."

The relationship between doña Jesusa and doña Itzel was far from good until after Júbilo was born. Because of race. Doña Itzel was one hundred percent Mayan Indian and she disapproved of the mixing of her race's blood with doña Jesusa's Spanish blood. For many years, she had avoided visiting her son's home. Her grandchildren grew up without her being very involved in their lives. Her rejection of her daughter-in-law was so great that for years she refused to speak to her, arguing that she couldn't speak Spanish. So doña Jesusa was forced to learn Mayan in order to be able to speak with her mother-in-law. But she found it very difficult to learn a new language while raising twelve children, so communication between the two was sparse and of poor quality.

But all that changed after Júbilo was born. As she desired with all her soul to be near the baby, his grandmother began to visit her son's house again, which had never happened with the other grandchildren, as if she had no great interest in them. But from the first moment she saw Júbilo, she became fascinated with his smiling face. Júbilo was a blessing to the family; he appeared like a gift from heaven that no one expected. A beautiful gift that they didn't know what to do with. The difference in age between him and the youngest of his siblings was several years, and a few of his older brothers and sisters were already married and had children of their own. So it was almost as if Júbilo were an only child, and his playmates were his nieces and nephews, who were the same age as he. Because his mother was busy simultaneously fulfilling the roles of mother, wife, grandmother, mother-in-law, and daughter-in-law, Júbilo spent a lot of time in the company of the servants, until his grandmother adopted him as her favorite grandchild. They spent most of the day together, taking walks, playing, talking. Of course, his grandmother spoke to him in Mayan, which meant that Júbilo became doña Itzel's first bilingual grandchild. And so, from the age of five, the child became the family's official interpreter. This was a fairly complicated matter for a small child, as he had to take into account that when doña Jesusa said the word *mar*, she was referring to the sea in front of their home, where the family often swam. On the other hand, when doña Itzel said the word *K'ak'nab*, she wasn't referring only to the sea, but also to the "lady of the sea," which is the name given to one of the phases of the moon and is associated with large bodies of water. Both of these entities have the same name in Mayan. So, as Júbilo translated, not only did he have to be aware of these subtleties, but he also had to pay attention to his mother's and grandmother's tone of voice, the tension in their vocal cords, as well as the expression on their faces and the set of their mouths. It was a difficult task, but one which Júbilo performed with great pleasure. Of course, he didn't always translate literally. He always added a kind word or two to soften the exchange between the two women. Over time, this little trick managed to help them get along a little better each day, and they eventually grew to love one another.

This experience helped Júbilo to discover the power of words for bringing people closer or pushing them apart, and that the important thing wasn't what was said, but the intention behind the communication. This sounds simple, but it is in fact very complicated. When Júbilo's grandmother gave him a message to translate, generally the words didn't coincide with what she really wanted to say. The tension around her mouth and vocal cords gave her away. Even to an innocent child like Júbilo, it was obvious that his grandmother was making an effort to swallow her words. But, as strange as it sounds, Júbilo heard the silent words clearly, even though they had never been spoken. And he understood that this "voice" that remained silent was the one that truly represented his grandmother's desires. So Júbilo, without thinking much about it, frequently translated those imperceptible murmurings instead of the words she spoke out loud. Of course, it never crossed his mind to do this to be naughty, just the opposite; his ultimate objective was always to reconcile these two women, both of them so beloved and important to him, to say out loud the magic word that neither of them ever dared to speak, the word that had to do with repressed desires. The frequent disagreements that arose between his mother and his grandmother were a clear example of this. Júbilo had no doubt that when one of them said black, she really meant white, and vice versa.

At his young age, what he didn't understand was why these two women made their lives, and as a consequence the lives of everyone around them, so complicated, since any argument between them had repercussions on all the rest of the family. There was never a strife-free day. They always found reasons to fight. If one said that Indians were lazier than Spaniards, the other would say that Spaniards smelled worse than Indians. There was no shortage of arguments, but without a doubt, the most sensitive were those that had to do with the life and customs of doña Jesusa. Doña Itzel had always worried that her grandchildren would be brought up in a life-style that, to her way of thinking, wasn't appropriate for them. This had been one of the main reasons why she had avoided coming to the house in the past. She had wanted to avoid seeing how her daughter-in-law was rais-ing the grandchildren like little Spaniards, but now she was back and was determined to save Júbilo, her favorite grandchild, from the loss of his cultural heritage. So he wouldn't forget his origins, she was always telling him Mayan stories and legends as well as accounts of the battles the Mayan Indians had been forced to fight to preserve their history.

The most recent was the War of the Castes, an Indian insurrection during which approximately twenty-five thousand Indians lost their lives, and in which as it happened Júbilo's grandmother herself had played an important role. In spite of the Indians' ultimate defeat, something good came out of that battle, because later her son Librado was placed in charge of one of the country's largest exporters of *henequén*—the fibers from an agave plant used for making rope and other materials. He had then taken the unusual step of marrying a Spanish woman. *Mestizaje*, the mixing of races, was not as com-mon in the Yucatán peninsula as it was in other regions conquered by the Spaniards. During the colonial period, Spaniards had rarely spent more than twenty-four hours at a time in the *encomiendas*, the large royal land grants where the Mayans worked as laborers. They didn't mix with the Indians and when they married they did so in Cuba, with Spanish women, never with Indians. So the marriage of a Mayan Indian man to a Spanish woman was highly unusual. But for doña Itzel this union represented a danger more than something to be proud of. And the proof lay in the fact that none of her grandchildren, except Júbilo, spoke Mayan, and that they preferred to drink hot chocolate made with milk instead of water. For anyone else, it would be amusing to hear the heated discussions these two women held in the kitchen, but not for Júbilo, because he had to translate for them. On these occasions he had to be even more attentive than usual, because he knew anything they said could easily be interpreted as a declaration of war.

One day the air in the kitchen was particularly heated. A couple of hurtful messages had already been hurled across the room, making Júbilo feel very uncomfortable, especially because the unhappiness his grandmother's words caused his mother was obvious. Most unbelievable, though, was that neither woman was really fighting about how to make hot chocolate. That was just a pretext. What doña Itzel was really saying was: "Look, *niña*, for your information, my forefathers built monumental pyramids, observatories, and sacred temples, and they knew about astronomy and mathematics way before your people, so don't you come trying to teach me anything, especially not how to make hot chocolate."

And doña Jesusa, who had a sharp tongue, had to repress the urge to counter: "Look, woman, you are used to looking down on anyone who is not of your race, because the Mayans are so great and so wonderful, but they are separatists by nature and I'm not about to put up with that kind of snobbishness. If you disdain me so much, then don't come to my house anymore."

Finally the situation grew so tense, and each woman was defending her point of view with such passion, that Júbilo began to fear something terrible would happen. So when his mother, summoning up her courage, said: "Son, tell your *abuela* that I don't allow anyone to come into my house to tell me how to do things, because I don't take orders from anyone, especially not from her!" Júbilo had no choice but to translate: "*Abuela*, my *mamá* says that we don't take orders in this house . . . well, except from you."

UPON HEARING THESE WORDS, doña Itzel changed her attitude completely. For the first time in her life, she felt her daughter-in-law had acknowledged her rightful position. Doña Jesusa, on the other hand, was taken by surprise. She never imagined her mother-in-law would react to such strong aggression with a peaceful smile. After the initial shock she too responded with a smile and, for the first time since her marriage, she felt accepted by her mother-in-law. With just a simple change of meaning, Júbilo had been able to give each of them what they had been seeking: to feel appreciated.

From that day on, doña Itzel, convinced her orders were now being followed to the last letter, stopped interfering in the kitchen; and doña Jesusa, confident that her mother-in-law finally accepted her way of life, was able to approach her *suegra*, her mother-in-law, affectionately. The whole family returned to normal thanks to Júbilo's mediation, and he in turn felt completely satisfied. He had discovered the power of words and, having acted as his family's translator since his early childhood, it wasn't too surprising that instead of wanting to be a fireman or a policeman, he expressed the desire to become a telegraph operator when he grew up.

This idea crystallized one afternoon as Júbilo lay in his hammock next to his father, listening to him talk. The Mexican Revolution had ended several years earlier, but all kinds of stories were still circulating about what had happened during the war. That afternoon the topic was telegraph operators. Júbilo listened eagerly to his father. Nothing gave him greater pleasure than to wake up from his compulsory siesta to hear his father's stories. The tropical heat forced the family to sleep in hammocks installed at the rear of the house, where there was a breeze from the ocean. There, beside *K'ak'nab*, they rested and talked. The gentle rhythm of the waves had carried Júbilo off into a deep sleep and the murmur of conversation brought him back in a delicious ebb and flow. Little by little, his father's words intruded upon his sleep and made him aware that he was back at home and that it was time to exercise his imagination. So, setting his tropical drowsiness aside, he rubbed his eyes and devoted himself to listening intently to his father.

Júbilo's father had just begun telling a story he'd heard about General Pancho Villa and his corps of telegraph operators. It has been said that the importance Villa always gave to telecommunications was one of the key factors in his success as a military strategist. He was well aware that it was a powerful weapon and he was very adept at its use. An example of this was the unusual way he used the telegraph in his siege of Ciudad Juárez. Because of its strategic location, the border city was an important stronghold, and it was very well provisioned. Villa didn't want to attack the city from the vulnerable position of the open desert, and he couldn't cross the border for a better approach, so he decided to capture a coal train on its way from Chihuahua to Ciudad Juárez and use it as a kind of Trojan horse. He loaded his troops onto the train and when they reached the first station along the route, they seized the official telegraph operator and replaced him with Villa's own head telegraph man, who sent a telegram to the *federales* saying: "Villa is pursuing us. What should we do?" Their answer was: "Return to Ciudad Juárez as fast as you can." And that's just what Villa's men did. The coal train arrived in Ciudad Juárez at dawn. The *federales* allowed it to enter the city and by the time they realized that instead of coal the train was filled with armed men, it was too late. And Villa was able to take Ciudad Juárez with a minimum of bloodshed.

They say a good listener requires few words. All Júbilo needed to hear his father say was, "Without the help of his telegraph operator, General Villa would never have won!" In Júbilo's mind, the image of the telegraph operator immediately grew to heroic proportions, that unknown soldier whose name no one even knew. If that man was admirable in his father's eyes, then he wanted to be a telegraph operator, too! He wanted to stop having to compete with his eleven older siblings. They were many years ahead of him, and had done a lot more studying. If his brothers weren't lawyers, they were doctors; if his sisters weren't beautiful dancers, they were brilliant thinkers. All of them were loaded with virtues and could claim multiple talents and abilities. Júbilo somehow believed that his father preferred talking to his brothers and sisters than to him, that he liked their jokes better than his, that he valued their achievements over those of his youngest son.

Feeling ignored and wanting to stand out any way he could, he dreamed of being a hero in his father's eyes, and what better way to achieve that than by becoming a telegraph operator? Júbilo knew he possessed a special gift for hearing and transmitting messages, so the work couldn't be that hard. He yearned desperately to be a telegraph operator. What did one need to do to become one? Where did one study? For how long? The questions shot from his mouth like skillfully aimed bullets and the answers came back just as quickly. What excited him most was finding out that to be a telegraph operator, one had to learn Morse code, a mode of communication that very few people knew. Everything was looking great! Since only he would know what was said to him in the messages that he was to transmit, he would be able to translate them in his own way! He could already see himself appeasing lovers, arranging weddings, and ending all kinds of animosities. Without a doubt, he was going to become the best telegraph operator in the world. He felt it from the bottom of his heart. And the proof lay in the way he had repaired the relationship between his mother and his grandmother. Mastering Morse code couldn't be any more complicated than that. Besides, he felt he possessed a gift. He knew perfectly well that his ability to "hear" people's true feelings wasn't shared by everyone. What Júbilo wasn't then able to see, however, was that his greatest gift would, over the years, become his greatest misfortune, that being able to listen to unrepeatable secrets, wishes, and desires wasn't as wonderful as it seemed, that being aware of what other people felt at every moment would come to cause him a lot of headaches, and huge disappointments in love. But in that early moment of laughter and happiness, who was going to tell Júbilo that life was difficult? Who could have warned him that he would end up lying in bed, in a near vegetable state and incapable of communicating with those around him? Who?

"¡HOLA JUBIÁN! HOW ARE YOU?"

"Well, I am . . ."

"*Mi compadre,* you look pretty good to me."

"Well . . . I . . . can't . . ."

"What's the matter, do I look that bad?"

"No, don Chucho, what my father means is that he can't see you, not that you look bad, you just didn't let him finish."

"I'm sorry, *compadre.* You speak a little slowly and I got ahead of myself."

"That always causes problems. The other day Aurorita, his nurse, asked him if he wanted to go to the dining room to eat, and my father said yes, but first he wanted to go to the bathroom. So Aurorita helped him into his wheelchair, took him to the bathroom, helped him to his feet, and started to open his zipper. Then, slowly, my father said, 'No . . . I just want . . . to wash my hands. . . .' Aurorita laughed and said, 'Ay, don Júbilo, then why did you let me open your zipper?' And my father answered, 'Well, because I thought you had good intentions!'"

"*¡Ah, mi compadre!* You haven't changed, have you?"

"Ha . . . ha . . . No . . . why should I?"

"Listen, don Chucho. Was my father always such a joker?"

"Always . . . right, Jubián? He's been like that ever since I met him."

"And when was that?"

"Oh, I don't even remember, I think your father was about nine and I was about six. He had just arrived from Progreso, I think, because the export company where your grandfather worked had closed down. But I can still see in my mind what he looked like the first time I saw him, newly arrived from the train station, standing there next to his suitcase. I remember noticing that he was wearing short pants, like a little sailor and, well, let me tell you! All the kids in the neighborhood started making fun of him. We asked him if he'd lost his ocean. And where the costume party was. You know, kid stuff."

"And what did my father do?"

"Nothing. He just laughed along, and said, 'There's no costume party, but didn't anybody tell you that I brought the ocean along with me?' He pointed behind us. 'Look, there comes a wave!'

"And like young fools, we all turned around to look, and your father just laughed. From that moment I liked him, and our friendship just grew. We lived on Calle Cedro; your *papá* lived in number fifty-six, and my family was across the street, so we spent our days together. We were never apart. And when my family moved to Calle Naranjo, Júbilo would come over as soon as he got home from school. We loved to play in the street; back then there was no danger of getting run over, because cars only came by every now and then, and buses, never! Life was very different then and the neighborhood was beautiful, but now, well, you can't go out at night because you'll get attacked. Like they did to me. I even had to go to the hospital. It's so unsafe that the drugstore on the corner—remember it, Jubián?—well, now it has bars on the windows to prevent robberies. I remember when the González girls lived upstairs and at night your father and I would go to see if we could watch them undress when they went to bed. You're listening to me, aren't you, Jubián? I'm going to take advantage of the fact that you can't talk back: I'm going to tell your daughter some stories, you're not going to sock me, are you?"

"Ha, ha. I . . . wish . . . I . . . could."

"I don't doubt it for a minute! The only advantage I now have over you is that you can't move, 'mano, otherwise . . . ! Did you know that your *papá* had a great boxing arm?"

"No."

"Man, was he good! One day he even landed a punch on Chueco López, a boxer from those days, who was after your *mamá's* bones."

"Really?"

"Sure. We had a party one evening, back when we lived on Calle Naranjo, and the three of us were out on the balcony. Chueco climbed up a pole just to see your *mamá;* your *papá* gets so mad he picks a fight with the guy, and wins!"

"But why was he so angry? Was he already dating my mother?"

"No, not at all, I had just introduced them. No, according to Jubián the problem was that Chueco had shown your *mamá* disrespect, but the truth is I was there too, Jubián, and I never heard anything that sounded like an insult...."

"He didn't say it out loud ... but ... he thought it...."

"Ha, ha, ha ... Oh Jubián!"

"So, don Chucho, you introduced my parents?"

"Yes, and your father still hasn't forgiven me. Right, *compadre?*"

"Noooo..."

"Ha, ha, ha ... it's time you forgave me, it was all your own fault after all. That night, instead of hitting Chueco, you should have gotten out of his way, so that he could have married Lucha instead and you'd be singing a different tune now...."

"How could I ... do that ...? I liked the guy!"

"Ha, ha, poor Chueco López, he was a good guy. He taught me how to box. He was a great boxer, he even made it to the Arena México and the Arena Libertad. Because I was little, they used to pick on me at school, so I asked him to show me how to fight and he said yes. He had a punching bag and a boxing ring in his basement, where he gave me my first lessons. He told me the main thing in boxing is never to close your eyes, because that's when they get you. That's why I told Jubián, '*Mira compadre*, when Lucha hits you, don't ever close your eyes,' but he never listened to me.... Oh well, that's life. Poor Chueco had a rough life too. He really liked to drink and he ended up as a *jicarero* in a bar, a *pulquería*...."

"What's a *jicarero?*"

"Someone who serves pulque, similar to tequila, from a *jícara*, or gourd. But that was in the old days—they don't do it that way anymore. Everything's changed. . . . Well, Chueco died, but we're still hanging on . . . that's why I try to get along as best I can while there's still life in me. I go bowling now, I really like it. I go three times a week. My bowling friends are all over sixty but they're still at it. There's one guy who just turned ninety, he's still bowling. And he's good, too. Imagine that! To still be able to handle a ten-pound ball at his age! The bad thing is they have started to charge eighty pesos a game, which is pretty expensive for us, given our pensions, it's just too much. But the good thing is that the other day, by chance, I was walking down Calle Sullivan and discovered a bowling alley above a shoe store. A man and a young girl were playing and I asked them if I could join in. They said the alley was set aside in the mornings for federal government retirees and I told them I was retired, but not from the federal government. They said it didn't matter, I could still play there. They usually charge eighteen pesos a game, but they let us senior citizens play for nine pesos, and they throw in free coffee too. And since I'm in with the owner of the restaurant, she always gives me two or three cups, because I take her a box of chocolates every now and then, you know? So she treats me pretty well. I've been playing for about thirty years and though I'm not that good, I'm not that bad either, I'm okay, I can't complain. My average score for a set of three games is between 150 and 160, even though sometimes I break out and get up into the five hundreds. A couple weeks ago I got 583 in three games! How do you like that, Jubián!? Jubián, have you stopped talking to me?"

"No, don Chucho, he just gets like that sometimes. He gets tired, or something, mostly when we talk about my *mamá*."

"That's a shame. Has she come to visit him?"

"No, she hasn't wanted to."

THIS LAST PART I say with some fear. Almost secretively. Aware of the way my father's ears have been trained to listen to two conversations at once. His gaze seems lost in his memories, but I know perfectly well that is no impediment for him to be able to follow the course of our conversation as well. His long years of practice as a telegraph operator allow him to handle two and even three conversations simultaneously with startling ease.

And I really don't want him to know my mother's opinion of him and his illness. Although, on the other hand, he's probably aware of *her* most recent thoughts, even though he hasn't looked her in the eyes for more than fifteen years. I wonder what image of my mother will remain with him? The one from the day they said good-bye? Or the day they first saw each other? Perhaps the image of her that day on that balcony, awakening all sorts of illusions and desires in the men around her, all admiring her figure. And my *mamá*, what image of her husband has remained with her? Is she capable of imagining my father as sick as he is? In the afternoons, after watching her *telenovelas*, does she ever think of him? And if she does, what image comes to mind? Above all, I wonder if she is capable of imagining him smiling, as he did in the good old days, when they danced *danzón* in the Plaza de Veracruz, when the magnet of the north caused the tide to rise in the eyes of the sea.

Chapter 2

DANZÓN MUSIC FLOODED the Plaza de Veracruz. Grace-
ful couples swept across the dance floor with swan-
like elegance, their bodies radiating sensuality with
every step. You could cut the voluptuousness in the air
with a knife. One couple stood out from all the rest, the
one comprised of Júbilo and his wife. Júbilo was wearing
a white linen suit and Luz María, his wife, a crisp white
organza dress. The whiteness of their clothes stood out
against their tanned skin. They had spent a month going
to the beach, daily, and it showed. The heat of the sun,
trapped within their bodies, now escaped in waves of
ardor, passion, and lust.

Luz María, affectionately called Lucha, swayed her
hips gently, but with Júbilo's heightened sensibilities, his
hand amplified her movement and it washed over him
like an effervescent wave, hot, joyful, dissolute, raising his
body temperature. Accustomed to transmitting telegraph messages at an extraordinary speed, Júbilo's fingers
appeared to rest innocently on the small of his wife's
back, but they were far from inactive, they were con-

stantly monitoring the movement, the fever, the desire hidden beneath her skin. Like voracious antennae, his fingertips captured the electric impulses from Lucha's brain, as if her thought waves were sending the order to follow the rhythm of the music directly to him. Lucha didn't need words to tell her husband how much she loved and desired him. Words travel as swiftly as desire, so it is possible to send a message of love without them. The only requirement for intercepting them is a sensitive receptor, and Júbilo certainly had that. He had been born with it buried deep within his heart. And with it he could decipher any number of messages originating from any other heart, regardless of whether the other person wanted to make them known or not. Júbilo had the ability to intercept these messages before they were converted into words. On many occasions, this gift had caused him problems, since people aren't accustomed to expressing their true intentions. People hide their feelings from others, often behind pretty words, or silence them to avoid violating social conventions.

The discordance between desires and words causes all kinds of communication problems and gives rise to a double standard both in individuals and in nations, who say one thing, yet do another. Ordinary people, who generally guide themselves by words, become totally confused when someone else's actions conflict with his statements. They feel out of control when they discover this contradiction, but curiously these same people prefer to be seduced rather than to feel deceived. They would more readily accept an outright lie than listen to Júbilo's assertions about someone's true intentions. It was normal for Júbilo to be called a liar when he spoke the truth.

Fortunately, at this particular moment, the electrical impulses coursing through his wife's body required only a simple interpretation, since they were totally congruent with what she was thinking and coincided completely with Júbilo's own desires. The way their bodies kept rhythm as they danced foretold the pleasure waiting for him later when they got home. The couple had only been married for six months and had done little more than explore, kiss, love one another in each of the small communities where Júbilo, as an itinerant telegraph operator, was sent to cover the vacations of the local operators. He was working in the beautiful city of Veracruz, and the amorous couple was grateful. Júbilo's new assignment seemed custom-made for them, particularly for Júbilo, who really needed a rest after the exhausting events of the previous months. Swimming in the ocean, walking on the salty sand, breathing in the smell of fish cooking, and lingering at the Café La Parroquia were the ideal revitalizing tonic for him, much more effective than the "Emulsión de Scott" that Lucha regularly dosed him with. And the sound of the seagulls, the handheld fans, and the breaking waves brought him great peace and took him back to the happy days of his childhood. Immersed in these familiar smells and sounds, he felt once again that life was pleasant and that he had no greater obligation than making love to his wife. Though, to be honest, he had to admit he couldn't think of anything but sex, whether he was in Veracruz or in Timbuktu. Even at work.

As he sent telegraph messages, he invariably thought of the way his fingers would caress the intimate recesses of Lucha's body. The way they would play with her clitoris and send her messages in Morse code, which, though she didn't completely understand them, were sufficiently explicit for her to respond with frenzied passion. Júbilo's mind simply couldn't be completely diverted away from his work, but nor could his work be separated from his loving. He argued that this was because these two activities were intimately linked.

To begin with, both needed an electric current in order to function. The telegraph machines obtained it from power lines, but in small pueblos where there was no electricity, the telegraph still functioned thanks to glass cylinders about fifteen inches tall and about six inches in diameter, which were filled with chunks of sulfur and water. A copper coil with two contacts would be placed in the top of the jar: one was for the water and the other for the copper coil, one positive and the other negative. The jars worked like Volta batteries and grouped together they provided the necessary voltage. Júbilo's theory was that the vagina functioned in a similar way, it contained fluid and was of an adequate size to produce, upon entering into contact with the male member (which could be compared to a sophisticated copper coil), a strong electrical current, just like a battery. The good, or bad, thing, depending upon how one looked at it, was that the battery only lasted a short while for Júbilo, and he regularly needed to plug himself back in to recharge his batteries. Lucha and he would rise early and make love, then Júbilo would go to work, send a few messages, and return to eat lunch. After eating, he would make love, then return to work. In the afternoon, he would transmit more messages, then go home again. In the evening, they would go out for a walk, have dinner, and before going to sleep they would make love again. Now that they were in Veracruz, the only variation in their routine was that they took time each day to go to the beach. But that was basically their entire life as newlyweds.

Though things had started to change a bit lately. That is not to say that the time between amorous interludes had grown longer, or that his wife's pregnancy had interfered with their sex life. Yet Júbilo felt there was an interference that disturbed the exchange of energies between them. He didn't know how to explain it, but he sensed that Lucha was hiding something from him. It was a thought she didn't dare to express and that Júbilo was unable to read, but he could feel it in his veins. This is best explained if one takes into account that a thought is an electric current, and water is one of the best conductors of electricity. Since there is an abundance of this element pumping through our bloodstream, it wasn't at all difficult for Júbilo to "feel" his wife's thoughts during the exchange of energies produced by their sexual inter-course. His wife's womb was his energy receptacle, as well as his power company, and lately he had suffered a change in voltage. It made Júbilo despondent, but when he questioned Lucha about it, she denied anything was wrong. Since he didn't have a device like a telegraph machine at hand to capture her hidden thoughts, he was forced to speculate about them. Of course, instead of guessing, he would have loved to be able to convert those electrical impulses into words. If only he could find a way to do that! If he could somehow invent a thought decoder. To his way of thinking, thoughts were entities that existed from the moment they originated in the mind; they consisted of waves of energy that traveled silently and invisibly through space until they were captured by some sort of receiving apparatus and converted into sounds, written words, or even images. Júbilo was convinced that some day an apparatus would be invented that would be able to convert the thoughts of others into images. There was nothing to prevent it. Meanwhile, he would have to keep using the only reliable receiving system he had at hand, which was himself. Maybe he only needed to fine-tune his perception a bit to capture the more subtle wavelengths, allowing him to expand his ability to communicate with the world around him.

Júbilo firmly believed that everything in the universe had a soul, that every single thing had feelings, thoughts—from the tiniest flower to the farthest galaxy. Everything had a particular way of vibrating and of saying, "Here I am." So it could be said that the stars talked, that they were capable of sending signals to indicate their most intimate thoughts. The ancient Mayans believed the stars were linked to the mind of the sun, and that if one managed to establish contact with the king of the stars, it was possible to perceive not only the sun's thoughts, but also its desires. And Júbilo, as a worthy descendant of that wonderful race, liked to open his consciousness and widen his sensibilities to embrace the sun, the stars, and a galaxy or two, trying to find a signal, a message, a meaning, a pulsing vibration that would speak to him.

How sad it would be if no one received those impulses! If no one understood them! If the emitted signals wandered aimlessly through the darkness of time. There was no thought that could disturb Júbilo more than a message that finds no receiver. Being such a wonderful listener, and having been born with the ability to interpret any kind of communication, he would feel depressed when a message languished without a response, floating there in space, unnoticed. Like a caress that never touches skin, or a freshly fallen fig which is ignored, uneaten, and ends up rotting on the ground. There was nothing worse, thought Júbilo, than the idea of countless messages that never knocked on a door and just languished in space, disoriented, wandering, unclaimed. How many of these pulsating, invisible, inaudible presences were spinning around a person, a planet, or the sun? This simple thought filled Júbilo with guilt. It made him miserable, as if it were his responsibility to receive messages for all those who couldn't. He would have loved to tell everyone that he was able to perceive their signals, that he valued them and, most important, that they were not sent in vain. Over the years he found the best way to acknowledge the signals of others was by fulfilling their most intimate desires, by doing them an honest act of service.

Perhaps this sentiment was born one distant day when his grandmother took him into the jungle, to a secret place, a hidden Mayan stela still undiscovered by archaeologists. To the eyes of a small boy, it seemed like a colossal monument, difficult to take in at first. Just as great was its power of attraction. The hieroglyphics carved into the stone instilled a tremendous fascination in all those who gazed upon it. Doña Itzel and Júbilo studied it for a long time while the old woman smoked a cigarette. It was one she had fashioned herself, the tobacco wrapped in a corn husk. We're talking about a whole leaf of the husk, so it was quite a cigarette and took doña Itzel a long time to finish. During this time, Júbilo concentrated on the hieroglyphics.

"What does it say, *abuela?*" he asked.

"I don't know, child. Apparently, some very important dates are written on this stela, but no one has been able to interpret them."

Young Júbilo was horrified. If the Mayans had bothered to spend so much time carving this stone to leave the dates inscribed on it, it was because they considered them to be truly important. How was it possible that they had been forgotten? He just couldn't believe it.

"But tell me, *abuela*, isn't there anyone who knows the numbers?"

"That's not the problem, Che'ehunche'eh Wich. We can read the numbers, what we don't know is the corresponding dates on our calendar, because the Mayan calendar was different, and we're missing the key that would allow us to interpret them."

"And who has it?"

"No one, it was lost during the *conquista*. As I have told you, the Spaniards burned many, many codices, so there are many things we will never know about our ancestors."

As doña Itzel took a long puff of her cigarette, a tear ran down young Júbilo's cheek. He refused to believe that so much had been lost. It couldn't be true. This stone slab spoke to him, and although he was unable to understand it, he was sure he could decipher its mystery, or at least he was going to try.

He spent days learning the Mayan number system, which is based on the number twenty and employs dots and lines for its written expression. Curiously, this training helped him, years later, when it came to learning Morse code. But at the time, he had no idea he was going to be a telegraph operator and his only concern was to find the hidden key that would allow him to decipher the Mayan dates. Nothing could have made doña Itzel happier. To see her grandson so completely absorbed in the culture of the ancient Mayans filled her with pride and satisfaction. And more important, I think that was what allowed her to die in peace, since she realized that her legacy on earth was assured in a member of the family. She was now certain that Júbilo would not forget his Mayan roots. She died peacefully, smiling. And while Júbilo was saddened by her death, he could find some comfort in it too. His grandmother died at the right time, before modern development could scandalously overtake Progreso, her quiet pueblo. It was indeed ironic that his grandmother had lived in a town named Progreso, because although she was an active woman with liberal ideas, she in no way shared the urge for progress that was so common at the time. She accepted that women could smoke and fight for their rights, she even supported the 1916 movement to regulate abortion in the Yucatán. But she was adamantly opposed to the advent of the telegraph, the telephone, the train, and all other modern technological advances, which in her mind only caused people's heads to fill with noise, made them live more frenetically, and distracted them from their true interests.

In some way, his grandmother saw all these advances as crude successors of the positivist thought that defined the *Científicos*, a group of misguided characters who had kept President Porfirio Díaz in power for many years. It was during Díaz's dictatorship, in 1901, that the book *Mexico: Its Social Evolution* was published. Written by the positivist doctor Porfirio Parra, the book was a clear testimony of what the day's most respected and refined authorities really thought about Mexicans. In a single stroke, this book disowned Mexico's Indian heritage, leaving it out of the story completely. Parra claimed that before the arrival of the Spaniards, the Indians only knew how to count up to twenty, and that their mathematical knowledge only extended to life's bare necessities and was never used for scientific investigation. According to Parra, the origins of Mexican science lay in the facts imported by the conquistadores, not in any native knowledge. It was a history charged with racist undertones, not to mention ignorance, and it justified doña Itzel's fear that all these recent technological advances would obscure the fight to break away from *Cientificismo*'s legacy and to return to true Mexican, Indian, values being mounted by great Mexicans, like José Vasconcelos, Antonio Caso, Diego Rivera, Martín Luis Guzmán, and Alfonso Reyes.

For doña Itzel, it was clear that the real question surrounding the issue of the train lay not in whether one would be able to reach his destination more quickly, but in why he would want to. The danger she saw was that technological advances served no purpose if they were not accompanied by an equivalent spiritual development. Even though they had gone through a revolution, Mexicans had not acquired any greater consciousness of who they were. And now, living even faster than before, how were they to connect with their past? When were they going to stop wanting to be what they weren't?

His grandmother died without finding the answer to these questions, and Júbilo, though visibly affected by her death for quite some time, never stopped trying to decipher the enigma of the hieroglyphics. His mathematical studies finally led him to the key to the Mayan calendar. All the wisdom achieved by the amazing Mayan astronomers was locked within thirteen numbers and twenty symbols. The Mayans were acutely aware of the skies that surrounded them and the movement of the planets. Not only could they predict eclipses with great precision, but they could also calculate Earth's orbit around the sun with an accuracy to within a thousandth of a decimal point of the calculations of modern science. How could this be explained in a civilization that didn't have modern instruments of measurement? That hadn't even reached the point of discovering the use of the wheel as a means of transportation?

Júbilo arrived at the conclusion that it was because the Mayans were able to establish an intimate connection with the universe that surrounded them. They used the term *Kuxán Suum* to define the way we are connected with the galaxy. *Kuxán Suum* translates as "The Way to the Sky That Leads to the Universe's Umbilical Cord"—a line that extends from the solar plexus of each man and passes through the sun until it reaches the *Hunab-Kú*, which translates as "The Beginning of Life Beyond the Sun." For the Mayans, the universe was not separated or atomized. They believed that a subtle web of fibers maintained a constant connection between certain bodies. In other words, that the galaxy was integrated in a resonating matrix, within which the transmission of information occurred instantaneously. And that any individual who had the necessary sensitivity to perceive the resonance of specific objects could connect with them and enjoy immediate access to all cosmic knowledge. He could perceive the resonance of objects. Of course, when the *Kuxán Suum* became obscured we could not connect with anything, since our own resonance was diminished, and although the sun could be right in front of us, it wouldn't say anything to us.

It was very interesting to imagine the galaxy as a resonating box. To resonate means to echo. And to echo means to vibrate. The whole universe pulses, vibrates, echoes. Where? In objects equipped to receive energy waves. Júbilo discovered that pointed objects were more efficient for receiving energy than rounded objects. So the construction of pyramids by his ancestors, as well as the raising of telegraph posts by his contemporaries, seemed completely logical to him.

His understanding of this phenomenon provided him with an explanation for his having been born with a pointed skull, which acted as a powerful antenna and served marvelously for connecting with the cosmos. And for his erect member, which connected him with the deepest and most sonorous matrix in the world: his wife's. This was the basis of Júbilo's ability to establish a strong connection with people, even across distances. More surprisingly, he could connect with objects too, and even with something as abstract as numbers. A possible explanation for this lay in that Júbilo, being a high-frequency antenna, not only intercepted subtle vibrations from all things but also was in complete harmony with them. In other words, he not only perceived the vibrating waves but became one with them, vibrating at the same rate and frequency. Like the sound of a guitar cord being strummed and then echoed by another cord tuned to the same note. The second cord, even though it hasn't been touched, will vibrate at the same time as the first. For Júbilo, echoing was the best way to respond to a vibration that said, "Here I am." It was his way of saying, "Here I am too, and I am vibrating right along with you."

And so it wasn't so strange that Júbilo could communicate with numbers. In his extensive study of Mayan numerology, he had discovered that writing the number five wasn't the same as writing the number four. And not just because they represented a different accumulation of elements, but because each number had its own distinct way of resonating, just like a musical note. So, just as he could clearly recognize the difference between do and re, Júbilo could also determine with great precision the number of a playing card lying facedown on a table. This made him an exceptional card player, but, curiously, he rarely played, and never with his friends, because it seemed dishonest to him to take advantage of his ability to connect with numbers. The only time he made an exception was in Huichapan, a tiny, peaceful pueblo in the Sierra de Puebla, when he was standing in for the local telegraph operator who was on vacation.

A persistent rain had fallen all day. The houses had

wide eaves so people could walk along the narrow streets without getting wet. The climate induced a sort of melancholy that clung to the bones of the pueblo's inhabitants and was much worse than the constant dampness. In the two weeks that Júbilo and Lucha had been in the town, Júbilo hadn't felt the slightest urge to explore this popular tourist destination. He preferred spending his free time frolicking in bed with his wife. But one afternoon, one of his most frequent telegraph clients, a young local named Jesús, had come to send his regular telegraph to Lupita, his girlfriend, who lived in the city of Puebla. Lupita and Jesús were getting married in two weeks. The preparations for the wedding were already well along and Júbilo had been sending a flurry of telegrams to the bride-to-be informing her of the details of the religious ceremony, how many flowers and candles would adorn the church, the number of chickens that would be sacrificed for the banquet, in short, Júbilo even knew how many kisses Jesús was planning to give her and, most important, where. Of course, this last bit of information had not been divulged by the groom-to-be. But it had been present in his mind and Júbilo, without wanting to, had simply received the confidential message while he was watching Jesús write his telegrams, which made him an unwitting accomplice to Jesús's love affair.

But that morning, as soon as he saw Jesús walk in the door of the telegraph office, Júbilo knew something serious had happened. Jesús entered with his head hanging, sad and distressed. Because his sombrero was tilted, rainwater ran off it, soaking the papers on the desk without Jesús even noticing. It seemed that he had even forgotten his good manners, because he didn't bother to remove the sombrero from his head. Timidly, Júbilo rescued a few forms from disaster and moved them out of harm's way while Jesús made several attempts to write a telegram that invariably ended up in the trash can. It was clear to Júbilo that whatever Jesús had to tell Lupita, it was certainly not pleasant. Wanting to help him, Júbilo spoke to the lovesick youth, little by little winning his confidence, until he finally got Jesús to confess his problem.

It turned out that Jesús was a hardened poker player and usually played at the cantina on Friday nights. But the previous week he had made a fatal decision. He had changed the day of his game from Friday to Saturday, to make the most of his last days as a bachelor, with disastrous results. He had lost everything. Everything! The *rancho* where he planned to live with Lupita, the money for the church, the banquet, the bride's dress, even the honeymoon trip that he had dreamed about for so long! It was obvious that the man was completely destroyed. Worst of all, he had lost his fortune at the hands of don Pedro, the local cacique, a landowning tyrant, a man who besides being rude, coarse, and evil-looking was abusive, exploitative, and a thief, among other charming traits.

Júbilo couldn't understand how it was possible that, knowing this about don Pedro, Jesús had still chosen to play with him—he simply couldn't believe it. Jesús tried to excuse himself by arguing that it had been impossible to avoid, that don Pedro had arrived at their poker table out of nowhere and asked if he could join the group, and none of them had been able to refuse. That was understandable. But what was still unclear was why Jesús had risked everything he had. Júbilo felt there must have been a very good reason. And while he listened to Jesús's long tale of woe, during which he blamed everything that had happened on an excess of alcohol, Júbilo focused on entering into harmony with Jesús's suffering to try to find the real answer. He discovered that what his friend was hiding behind his sad and glassy gaze was the flimsy hope of defeating, for once in his life, the man who had taken all of his family's possessions from them. This revelation certainly explained Jesús's irrational behavior. The feeling of injustice was so deeply buried within his soul that it made him feel totally powerless, the impotence of several generations of campesinos who had suffered terrible abuse at the hands of the large landowners. Júbilo was so in tune with Jesús's pain that he felt in his own body the offense, the humiliation, the impotence. And in that instant, he knew he had to avenge this poor man who didn't know how to tell his fiancée, just two weeks beforehand, that they had to suspend the preparations for their eagerly anticipated wedding. Especially since in just a few days' time Lupita was to leave Puebla, together with her family, to come to Huichapan, where Jesús's entire family was anxiously awaiting her.

How could he explain the situation? How could he apologize? Jesús couldn't find the right words. Júbilo convinced him that the sadness that had settled in his heart wasn't the best condition in which to try to communicate, even to write a complete sentence, so he sent Jesús home, promising to write it himself, and send the telegram on Jesús's behalf. And so he did, but of course he didn't cancel the wedding, rather he told Lupita, in Jesús's name of course, how much he loved her. He didn't think it was necessary to say anything else. At least for the moment. There was still a lot that could be done and he was convinced that Jesús's problem must have a solution. The only thing he needed was time, and since there wasn't much of that, he decided not to lose another minute, and began plotting his revenge.

If there was something Júbilo couldn't stand, it was the abuse of power. In the short time he had been living in the pueblo, he had already heard about all the unimaginable horrors don Pedro had committed. How he had deflowered young virgins, exploited his workers, stolen money from the campesinos, and rigged cockfights and, as Júbilo had just seen, poker games. Júbilo was so indignant that, despite being the most peace-loving person in the world, he began to rue the fact that don Pedro had survived the Mexican Revolution. It would have been so perfect if the *revolucionarios*, in midrevolt, had shot him in the head! They would have done society a great favor and, above all, it would have saved Jesús a lot of pain. But, because of the inefficiency of the *revolucionarios*, he had no other choice but to confront the scourge himself.

He waited impatiently until Saturday night, and went

to the cantina. At eight o'clock sharp he made his appearance and immediately headed for don Pedro's table, prepared to bet an entire month's salary and all of his savings. Don Pedro received him with open arms, like a vampire would a fifteen-year-old virgin. In Júbilo, he saw a fresh source of money.

It only took Júbilo a few hands to learn how don Pedro exercised his power at the table. If the first card dealt him was an ace, they were all screwed. Don Pedro had such self-control that many other players left the game prematurely, and one needed to have really cold blood to stay and play the high bets. To make matters worse, in addition to being a good player, don Pedro was very lucky. If someone laid down three of a kind, he would match it with a higher set. If someone had a straight, he would kill it with a flush. And on the rare occasions that he didn't have a good hand, he resorted to bluffing, placing a huge bet to make the other players think he had a strong hand. And in general, although they doubted his honesty, no one was prepared to pay to find out. They preferred to remain in doubt rather than lose the money in their pockets. It was very expensive to investigate the kind of game that don Pedro played. And the idea of defeating him was not stimulus enough to risk losing a large amount of money, since what was being risked at the moment of betting was one's personal fortune, modest as it might be.

Don Pedro didn't like to lose, so he drew upon any number of intimidation tactics to win, depending on the situation. And to make his choice even easier, he possessed the great skill of being able to read his opponent's reactions, no matter how subtle, in a fraction of a second. For example, if he saw a man hesitate before matching his bet, he knew he didn't even have a single pair and would seize the advantage. If, on the other hand, don Pedro saw the man was eager to cover the bet, he would conclude that he had a good hand, which warned him that he would have to be careful. And if his adversary not only set his chips on the table with a firm hand, but upped the bet, then he would refuse to go higher, he would fold. It was that easy. He never took risks. He never allowed himself to grow excited. He carefully calculated each bet and, of course, he always won.

Júbilo skillfully let him win the first few hands, even while holding a better hand. It didn't matter. The night was young and he wanted don Pedro to gain confidence over him. Don Pedro fell into the trap. After an hour of playing, he was more than convinced that Júbilo was a mediocre player who posed no real threat. Suddenly, Júbilo began to change the rhythm of the game. He took advantage of the fact that it was the turn of César, the pharmacist sitting on his left, to deal. This way, Júbilo would be the first to receive his cards, and he could clearly sense what they would be. They were waiting for the fifth cards to be dealt. It was don Pedro's last opportunity to place his bet. Each of the players had four cards on the table. Three faceup and one facedown. Don Pedro showed a jack, an eight, and a three, and had another jack facedown. Júbilo had a nine, a seven, and a king showing, and had another king facedown. Which meant he had the better pair, but don Pedro didn't know this. In an attempt to investigate, don Pedro raised his bet, expecting Júbilo, if he had a pair of kings, to match and raise, but he didn't. He knew that if don Pedro suspected he had a pair of kings, he would probably fold, and that was the last thing Júbilo wanted.

He desired with all his heart to tear don Pedro to pieces, and this was his chance. Júbilo limited himself to matching don Pedro's bet, and did so with some hesitation. That was the signal don Pedro needed to guess that Júbilo had only a ridiculous pair of nines. Don Pedro grew calm. The pot that had accumulated on the table was considerable, and he wanted it. Before the fifth card was dealt, don Pedro revealed his pair of jacks to force Júbilo to show his pair of nines, but Júbilo kept his king hidden, which forced César to deal the fifth card faceup. Júbilo was sure he was going to get another king, and that don Pedro was going to receive another jack, but he didn't care, because three kings would beat three jacks. When César dealt Júbilo's fifth card, a gasp of surprise arose around the table. The magnificent king fell in slow motion, before don Pedro's impassive gaze. From what he could tell, Júbilo, who was now showing a pair of kings, was hiding a pair of nines. He didn't like that at all. It put Júbilo's hand above his. He set down his cigar and concentrated on receiving his last card. Since he had four cards showing, this one would be facedown. Don Pedro picked

it up slowly and looked at it cautiously. He almost smiled
with joy when he discovered he'd been dealt another jack.
He now had three jacks! That meant he had won. He
should have bet against the pair of kings, but he didn't. He
passed. His pulse accelerated. He was already anticipating
his victory, and, without hesitating, bet ninety pesos. That
was what Júbilo was waiting for. He calmly matched the
ninety pesos, and raised the bet again with the last twenty
pesos he had left, the balance of his capital. Don Pedro
was surprised by Júbilo's audacity. He assumed that
Júbilo's inexperience had caused him to be overconfident
about his two pairs, preventing him from guessing the
truth, that Júbilo had another king in his hand. And so,
sure of his triumph, he calmly matched the bet, and
asked, according to protocol:

"What do I have to beat?"

"Three kings," replied Júbilo, laying his cards on the
table.

Don Pedro couldn't bear losing. He grew red with
anger and from that moment on he lost all compassion
for Júbilo. He used all the tricks he knew to try to wipe
him out. When Júbilo bet, he wouldn't follow. But when
don Pedro bet, Júbilo had the misfortune of holding a
good hand, and was forced to follow. Little by little, don
Pedro took back all of Júbilo's winnings. Júbilo began
playing badly. He was nervous. No matter how hard he
tried to concentrate, he couldn't see which card he would
receive next, much less what don Pedro was holding. He
couldn't understand it. He had lost his communication

with the numbers, and he was playing blind. His hands began to sweat and his mouth grew dry. In just a few hands, he had lost nearly all the money he had won, and was now betting the last pesos that he had left.

He had a pair of sevens on the table. Don Pedro didn't even have a pair showing. Júbilo had been dealt his last card, but his hand hadn't improved. He was left with just the pair of sevens. He had to wait for don Pedro to see his final card and place his bet, before knowing how he would fare. Don Pedro, in spite of not holding a pair, had cards that were higher than his, so any pair he could make would beat Júbilo's pair. After looking at his card, don Pedro said with great self-confidence:

"I'll bet all the money you've got left."

Júbilo hesitated. All the other players had folded, so if he didn't match the bet no one would know what don Pedro was holding. But don Pedro had bet against all the money Júbilo had left! It was obvious that he wanted to leave Júbilo stripped naked, since he obviously believed that the money Júbilo had on the table was all that he had in the world. Júbilo's mind tried to sort out all the options. There was a high probability that don Pedro was bluffing, but the only way to find out for sure was to pay up, since it seemed that he had lost his capacity to connect deeply with people and objects. So he matched the bet, only to discover, with a sudden stabbing pain in the heart, that don Pedro had a pair of jacks. Júbilo felt a cold chill run through his body. He had lost everything.

EVERYTHING. He had nothing more to bet. As don Pedro collected the chips, a cigar dangling from his mouth, he said:

"*Bueno, amigo, muchas gracias.* I guess you don't have anything else to bet, do you?"

"No."

"What about that little Packard of yours? Don't you want to bet that?"

Júbilo was suddenly paralyzed. He and Lucha had, in fact, arrived in the pueblo in a Packard, but the possibility of using it for a bet had never crossed his mind, since it didn't belong solely to him. It had been a wedding gift from his in-laws. Lucha came from a family with money, and the gift, in addition to being a clear indication of their love for their daughter, was made so that their "treasure" could travel more comfortably as she accompanied her husband through "dirty little pueblos." The car was worth approximately thirty-six hundred pesos. Now, without thinking twice, Júbilo said:

"All right, I'll bet the car!"

Don Pedro smiled. He had been dying of envy since he first saw Júbilo arrive in his pueblo. Because of the car, yes, but also because of Júbilo's beautiful wife. He eagerly desired both, and he felt Júbilo didn't deserve either of them. And now the opportunity had presented itself to make them both his. He quickly began to shuffle the cards, but Júbilo interrupted him.

"Except I don't want to play poker anymore," Júbilo

said. "I'll bet you the car, plus all the money on the table, that Kid Azteca, who is fighting right now in the World Welterweight Championship in Mexico City, will win."

The offer was very tempting for don Pedro, but the trouble was that the bet was beyond his control. His tricks couldn't affect the final result. He would be at the whim of chance. But since he was in the middle of a lucky streak and he had won that night more than ever before, he didn't hesitate, and accepted the bet. The only problem lay in the fact that the fight wasn't transmitted by radio, so there was no way to learn the outcome until the following morning, when the newspaper arrived. Since it was very late and there were only a few hours left before dawn, Júbilo suggested they count the money on the table, which turned out to be a veritable fortune, and that afterward they all go together to the train station to wait for the first train to arrive, which would bring the newspaper. As soon as they knew who had won, the winner would be given the money, and that would be the end of it.

Everyone present, including don Pedro, quickly approved the suggestion and they all went to the train station. The little band was demonstrably excited about the unusual bet and there were all kinds of comments and conjectures. There was no one there who didn't wish for Júbilo to win, since most of them hated don Pedro with a vengeance, and those who didn't got pretty close. Júbilo preferred to remain silent. He had separated himself from the group to enjoy a cigarette. His gaze was fixed on the horizon and his hands were in his pockets. His poker companions respected his right to solitude. They imagined the uncertainty must have been killing him. It never occurred to them that Júbilo was in that state because he was having a moral crisis.

Chucho, his close friend since childhood and fellow telegraph operator, lived in Mexico City and was a boxing fan. Chucho had gone to the fight that evening, and had informed Júbilo of the result via telegraph before Júbilo had left for the cantina earlier that night to play cards. Before making his bet, Júbilo had already known who had won the boxing match. He had bet on a sure thing. And now the guilt was killing him. Not because don Pedro didn't deserve a taste of his own medicine, but because he had broken the telegraph operator's oath of confidentiality. The only thing that calmed him was knowing that Lupita and Jesús would have the money for their wedding and that Lucha, his beloved wife, would only be able to chastise him for his late return home, but not for the loss of their Packard.

The feeling of depression weighing upon Júbilo prevented him from enjoying the exclamations of pleasure, the congratulations, the embraces of everyone gathered there. Their excitement was so great that the group suddenly lifted him up on their shoulders. The only one who wasn't thrilled with his triumph was don Pedro. As soon as he had read the result in the newspaper, he turned and walked away, swearing to himself. He didn't know how to lose. He had never learned how, and at fifty it was too late for him to learn. He swore that some day he would get even with Júbilo. The look don Pedro gave Júbilo before leaving the train station let him know that he now had an enemy for life. But Júbilo didn't care. He knew that in two weeks he would be transferred to Pátzcuaro and he was certain that he would never cross paths with don Pedro ever again. Júbilo had no idea that fate had other plans for both of them. But at that moment he couldn't think about anything other than being in Lucha's arms. He desperately needed to rest. He wanted to forget about the night and get back to his normal life, but it was too late. That night would become a watershed moment in his life.

Some of those present invited him to join them for a *birria*, a tripe stew, at the market to celebrate his victory, but Júbilo wasn't in the mood for it—he excused himself as politely as he could and turned to walk away. What was he supposed to be celebrating?! He felt like a total loser. He had lost his contact with numbers. He had failed as a receptive antenna. He had dishonored the profession of telegraph operator. He had failed everything that was most important in his life. Not even the sun could brighten him up now. And that wasn't just a figure of speech.

A light rain, the *chipi-chipi*, as the locals called it, softly soaked the streets. It didn't make any noise, but it was bothersome just the same. The dampness of the place couldn't have been any more in tune with Júbilo's mood. He felt an ache in his bones and in his soul. And the cloudy sky was itself an immense impediment to the alleviation of his suffering. It was so difficult for Júbilo not to be able to see the sun, not to be able to connect with it, not to be able to warm himself with its rays. Suddenly, as if the sky had taken pity on him, the clouds opened and allowed the first rays of sun to filter through. Júbilo immediately stopped in his tracks to enjoy the beauty of the sunrise. For many years he had made a habit of greeting the sun as part of his daily ritual. His grandmother had taught him to venerate the sun, and he had faithfully maintained the tradition, to the point that before he began his day he felt compelled to seek the great star's blessing. So Júbilo, with his arms raised high, now made his usual greeting, but unlike every other day, this time he didn't receive any response. The sun had stopped speaking to him. Júbilo believed that it was doing this to teach him a lesson. He knew he should never have used his ability as a mediator, as a receptor and communicator, for something so superficial as a game of cards. He should never have used confidential information for personal benefit. However, he did feel that the punishment he was receiving was exaggerated. He had recognized his mistakes, but he didn't think they were that grave. After all, this was the first time he had erred.

All this self-judging and speculation came purely out of Júbilo's own guilty conscience: it had nothing to do with reality. It wasn't true that the sun had stopped speaking to him, and even less true that it was punishing him. What was really happening was that the earth was being affected by atmospheric phenomena generated by the sun, and when there are a lot of visible sunspots, radio signals are distorted and are more difficult to receive. And in that year, 1937, the sun was in full activity, making it impossible for Júbilo to properly connect with it. The same phenomenon explained why he hadn't been able to intercept don Pedro's thought waves during the poker game, and why he often found it difficult to understand Lucha, a woman influenced by the magnet of the north and who suffered like no one else when sunspots appeared. Knowing this would have saved Júbilo a lot of problems. More than anything else, he would have understood that sometimes good intentions aren't enough to establish good contact with the cosmos. That with the presence of sunspots there would always be a loose connection somewhere, some broken communication, or some wandering desire unable to establish contact with its intended receptor and which was destined to become a misunderstood meteorite.

Unfortunately, Júbilo learned all of this years later, when he took a radio operator course for the Compañía Mexicana de Aviación, the Mexican Aviation Company. But, luckily, he didn't have to wait that long to find out that his capacity for receiving messages was still there, that it hadn't been completely lost. There in Veracruz, near the sea, near Lucha, near his Mayan ancestors, he realized it still worked. While he was dancing to the rhythm of that *danzón*, he received a message. It came from his wife. She had sent it through the movement of her hips, and Júbilo had understood it clearly. What happiness he felt! When there was no interference in communication! When a tiny click could produce a spark of understanding in the brain. A moment like this could only be compared to an orgasm. Lucha's hips, moving in cadence and marking the time of the timbal, seemed to be signaling to her husband in Morse code, "I love you, Júbilo, I love you, I love you . . ."

At that moment nothing else mattered, everything was perfect. The tropical heat, the music, the trumpet solo, the resonance of their hearts and desires . . .

"I WANT . . ."

"What do you want, don Júbilo? Do you want me to take your blood pressure?"

"I want . . ."

"No? Then do you want me to raise your head?"

"I want . . ."

"No? Then do you want the bedpan? Oh, I know, you want some water!"

"I want . . . to fuck!!"

"¡Ay! Don Júbilo, you're so crude! Why don't you just go back to sleep, close your eyes, go on. . . . What . . . ? You want me to turn up the music? All right, but just a little, because you won't be able to sleep well otherwise, and remember, your friends are coming to visit tomorrow, so you have to look your best."

Chapter 3

I T FEELS SO EXASPERATING to be with my *papi* and not be able to understand what he is saying. It's like looking at a Mayan stela that holds a whole world of knowledge inside, but is unintelligible to us profane souls. The afternoon light filters across his profile, outlining his strong Mayan features. His flat, sloped forehead, his aquiline nose, his recessed chin.

It has been a while since my *papá* turned his face toward the window in an attempt to escape. I imagine it must be unbearable for him not to be able to speak. His friends have just gone, and it has left a bittersweet flavor in the air. Probably more for my father than for me. Yet, these visits have turned out to be most revealing. They are showing me a father I never knew. A very different father from the one who taught me how to walk, who told me stories, who helped me with my homework, who always supported me. It is disconcerting to discover the real man behind that looming paternal figure. He is a strange and enigmatic man who spent the greater part of his productive life in the company of the people with whom he worked. A man capable of getting drunk, of shouting cat-calls, of flirting with a secretary or two. A man who was once an innocent child and liked to play ball on the broad Alameda de Santa María la Rivera. A man who in the spring of his youth had delighted in watching his neighbors undress. A man who so often had joked, eaten, danced, serenaded with these good friends, these people from whom we, his children, had somehow separated him without ever being aware of it. It is truly moving to see how they love and understand each another, to the extent that at some points during their visits I feel relegated to the background, excluded from the complicity that exists between them. A phrase is enough to make them laugh, to remember an important anecdote, to connect them in a profound way.

During their time in the house, I had a chance to observe them and to learn that behind the jokes and the laughter they were hiding great pain. They all made a tremendous effort not to show it, but it obviously grieved their souls to see my *papá* in this condition. They must fear the same thing happening to them. Reyes, who had not seen my father in a long time, almost burst out crying when he first set eyes on him. The memory he had of my *papá* was of a strong man, active and in full use of all his faculties. The contrast was hard to bear. I imagine it was difficult for him to accept that Júbilo the athlete or Júbilo the storyteller was no more. Before him was an extremely thin man, helpless in a wheelchair, who could barely speak and had completely lost his sight, but who fortunately still retained his sense of humor. Thanks to that, we were all able to overcome our sadness and spend a pleasant afternoon.

The presence of these beloved colleagues, his fellow telegraph operators, made it very clear that my father didn't belong exclusively to me. My *papá*, my beloved *papá*, is not mine alone. He belongs equally to these friends, to the downtown streets, to the Carrara marble stairs of the old telegraph building, to the sand of the beach where he learned to walk. He also belongs to the air, his favorite element, which he now misses the most, the same air that hasn't vibrated with the sound of his voice for such a long time now.

A few days ago my son and daughter-in-law visited. Federico and Lorena came to give their grandfather and me the wonderful news that they are going to be parents. The smile my *papá* gave us was a solid indication of what he thought of the news. After the hugs and congratulations, I grew sad when I realized my future grandson would never know the sound of my father's voice. This made me reflect upon how privileged I was to have been able to hear it, to have enjoyed his sustaining words. My father's voice! Only then did I begin to realize how much I missed it, how badly I needed to hear it, and that I had a responsibility to ensure that his voice reached the new generations and wasn't lost forever.

A few days ago, trying to find a lost echo, I went back

to my parents' old neighborhood. I looked for number 56 Calle *Cedro*, the first house where my father lived when he arrived in Mexico City, and I found a house as old and deteriorated as he was. The house's structural deterioration pained me deeply. How was it possible that no one was concerned about preserving our national heritage? That no one seemed to care about maintaining the fountain on the Alameda de Santa María, where my father learned to roller-skate? And the Moorish kiosk where my parents kissed for the first time? With a lump in my throat I walked through the Museo del Chopo, which I had done so many times before, holding my father's hand. I blessed the structure of iron and glass and steel, grateful that it had admirably withstood the passage of time. I remembered when it housed the Museum of Natural History, and there were glass cases where one could view an amazing collection of fleas dressed in costumes. For me, most memorable, besides the flea wearing a *china poblana*, the colorful traditional costume of Puebla women, was the bridal couple. The bride with her white dress, veil, and bouquet of flowers, the groom in his black suit and shiny black shoes. I would always say that they looked like my parents on their wedding day, to elicit a laugh from my father. I loved the way the sound of his laughter resonated in the museum's high glass nave.

Later I visited the mansion that for years was the home of the Colegio Francés, where my mother had studied. I leaned against a tree facing the main door, but on the other side of the street, just as I imagined my father must have done a thousand times as he waited for the exit of the "fine fillies," as he called the starched señoritas in their delicately embroidered navy blue uniforms with white collars, cuffs, and belts. And I don't know whether it was the nostalgia, the sadness, or perhaps both, but in that instant something resonated within me. I don't know how to explain it, but I couldn't help relating it to the texture, the tone, and the softness of my father's voice. It was an old voice, beloved and familiar. It was a nearly imperceptible murmur deep inside me, but I found it comforted me tremendously. I felt safe and protected as I had when I was a child, when my father would call me Chipi-chipi as he kissed me good night.

The bells in the tower of the Museum of Geology ringing six times broke my reverie. I suddenly remembered I had to get back and give my father something to eat. I quickly headed for the La Rosa bakery, which luckily was still there, and bought a few *conchas*, the sweet rolls my father loves so. When I arrived home, I prepared some hot chocolate as his grandmother would have done, with water, and in a wooden vessel, and we sat there drinking and eating and listening to a record by Los Panchos. And suddenly, in a quick burst, the image of my father singing those same songs came back to me. I remember my mother once telling me that my father had played in a trio, and that he and his friends would often serenade her. I wondered what had happened. Why had my father stopped playing the guitar? Why hadn't I ever heard him sing a love song? I would have to learn to listen to his silence to find the answers.

I feel that my *papá* is absent, submerged in his memories. It brings back an image I have recorded in my memory, of the afternoons when he would make himself a Cuba libre, and sit in his favorite chair to listen to his Virginia López record while he smoked his cigarette. In those moments I never liked to approach him. I felt it wasn't the right time. I feel the same way now. I think that after his friends' visit, he needs a little solitude. I am going to give it to him, and I'll ask his nurse also to take a few minutes' rest.

I too need to be alone. There's an idea I've been bouncing around in my head. During the visit today, there was a moment when my father grew so exasperated at not being able to express his ideas, that his friend Reyes improvised a telegraph machine so my *papá* could "talk" with his friends. The telegraph was nothing more than two spoons placed back to back, one on top of the other, so that when my father struck them together they produced a sound that could be interpreted by his telegraph-operator friends. The experiment hadn't worked perfectly, but it worked well enough to leave me with the hope that my father might still be able to communicate with us, that there was a key—Morse code— that could help me to decipher the mysteries inside that beautiful Mayan head.

My *mamá* always says that there is a reason for everything. Well, I would finally like to know the reason for my parents' separation. Why did they stop speaking to each other? What was it that my *papá* didn't want to see that made him blind? What was it that he was trying to hold in so forcefully that it gave him Parkinson's disease? What made these two guitar strings stop playing in harmony? When did these two bodies stop dancing to the same rhythm?

Chapter 4

L OVE IS A VERB. One demonstrates one's love through one's actions. And a person can only feel loved when someone else shows their love with kisses, hugs, caresses, and gifts. A lover will always promote the physical and emotional well-being of the person he loves.

No one would believe that a mother loved her child if she didn't feed him or take care of him, if she didn't clothe him when he was cold or help him develop and achieve independence.

No one would believe that a man loved his wife if, instead of providing her with money for household expenses, he threw it away on women and drink. When a man thinks first about satisfying the needs of his family, rather than his own, that is an act of love. Perhaps that is why a man who is able to do so is pleased when this is recognized, and feels so proud when his wife says, "Darling, I love the dress you bought me." Because those words confirm his ability to choose an appropriate gift, to pay for it, and, finally, to make his spouse happy.

So we see that the verb *to love* can be conjugated in

two ways. By hugging and kissing, or by supplying material goods. Providing food, clothing and shelter, and money for studies also translates into an act of love. We tell someone that we love him when we kiss him, or when we buy him the shoes that he so badly needs. And in this sense, the shoes serve the same function as the kiss. They are a token of our love. But this doesn't mean they can replace it. Without love, material goods can be a means of coercion or corruption, with which some people will seek to obtain the favors of others in return. And just as it is true that man cannot live by bread alone, he cannot survive by love alone either. Maybe that's why it's so sad to watch a poor man in love. No matter how successful a relationship may be, both sexually and emotionally, the lack of money can hamper and undermine, little by little, even the greatest passion.

Luz María Lascuráin, as the child of a well-off family, was accustomed to receiving all sorts of gifts and attentions. There was no toy Lucha couldn't have, no dress she couldn't wear, no food she couldn't eat. She was the youngest in a family of fourteen children and, needless to say, the most spoiled. She had everything she needed within her reach, and one might say even more. The Lascuráins always enjoyed great popularity in the neighborhood, due to the fact that they were the first family in the *colonia* to own a telephone, a Victrola, and, later, a radio. Lucha's father, don Carlos, was convinced that it was important to spend one's money on fitting into the modern world and on enjoying all the benefits that technology offered. He never scrimped a centavo on the purchase of any item that would make life at home more comfortable and pleasant, and his wife appreciated this.

Because of his money, he was able, among other things, to move his family from the northern part of the country to protect them from the dangers threatened by the Mexican Revolution. When Lucha was only a month old, they had moved to the capital, and spent the Revolution years safe inside the large Porfirian mansion don Carlos had purchased in Santa María la Rivera. So for the Lascuráin family, money represented security, peace, and opportunities for the children's education. With this background, it is understandable that to Lucha money seemed absolutely necessary, not only to live happily but also as a way of proving her love. She grew up observing how possessing capital ensured a family's happiness.

Júbilo's childhood was exactly the opposite. In his home, the lack of money never stopped his parents from showing their love for each other, nor indeed their love for their children. Despite having nothing more than the essentials, they were surrounded by love. After don Librado suffered a financial setback when the *henequén* exporting company he managed collapsed, he too had to leave his native town to move to the capital, but under conditions that were very different from the Lascuráins'. His savings soon ran out. His children had to attend public schools and had to go without luxury of any kind. Don Librado had to think carefully before making a purchase.

Júbilo never resented this, just the reverse. He was convinced that owning lots of clothing and furniture, far from bringing happiness, could turn people into the slaves of their possessions. He thought it was important to think very carefully before buying anything, because things required a certain amount of attention and over time they could become tyrants that demanded constant care. They had to be cleaned, protected, maintained; in short, he believed that possessions brought constraints, and he was too free-spirited to consider buying anything that would tie him down. He therefore also refrained from buying expensive gifts. First, because he didn't think it was a necessary requirement for showing his affection, and, second, because he was convinced that if he were to do so, he would also be giving enslavement, except for perishable gifts like flowers or chocolates. To his way of thinking, the true value of a present lay in what it meant to the donor, not in how much it cost. Money had no value for him and he would never dare compare it to a gesture of love.

For example, to Júbilo, arranging a serenade at three in the morning meant so much more than buying a diamond bracelet. It showed his willingness to forgo sleep, to withstand the cold, to run the risk of being mugged or getting drenched by irate neighbors. And that was certainly worth a lot more than simply a bought present. The value of things was so relative. And money, in his mind, was like a huge magnifying glass that only distorted reality and gave things a dimension they didn't really possess.

What was a love letter worth? In Júbilo's eyes, it was worth a great deal. So he was prepared to give away everything he held inside him to demonstrate his love. And it wasn't some kind of sacrifice, it came straight from his heart. To him, love was a life force, the most important thing he could ever feel. It was only when one felt its impulse that one could forget about oneself and think about someone else, and wish to be near her, touch her, become one with her. And for that, it wasn't necessary to have money. Desire was enough.

And he, better than anyone, knew that desires and words go hand in hand, that they are moved by the same intention to join together, to communicate, to establish bridges between people, whether they are spoken or written. Júbilo saw in every word the possibility of stepping outside of oneself in order to transmit a message to another human being. He preferred, of course, traveling words, words that crossed space, that reached far, even unimaginable, places. That was the reason the radio fascinated him so. The first time he heard a voice coming out of the apparatus it seemed like magic to him. It was in the house of his oldest brother, Fernando. He had bought the radio for his family, and Júbilo had been invited to the formal inauguration of the new invention by his nephews, who, curiously, were the same age as he was. The radio was large enough to accommodate eight pairs of headphones. Since speakers hadn't been invented yet, anyone who wanted to listen had to put on a headset and sit together with the others to share the experience. This meant the eight people sitting and listening to the same thing, at the same time, felt united in a very special way, and they would look at one another conspiratorially. It wasn't until Júbilo arrived in Mexico City that he learned how radios with speakers functioned. He would always remember the moment with tenderness, because the experience was the culmination of a very special day.

THE YEAR WAS 1923, and his father, don Librado, had decided to take him for a ride, to show him the city that was to be their new home. When Júbilo first arrived in the city, everything was new to him. He was mesmerized by it all. But more than anything else, he discovered loneliness for the first time. He missed the warm temperatures of his native land, the company of his nieces and nephews, the delicious southeastern food, and, above all, the accent of the people from the Yucatán peninsula. They spoke differently in the capital. Júbilo felt like a stranger in his own country. So he was very grateful to his father for giving him the opportunity to familiarize himself a little with his new city. He hired a *carretela*, and took Júbilo and his mother for a tour of the city in the open carriage. Soon, however, a steady rain began to fall and it lasted the entire ride. The driver used the canvas that usually covered the rear of the vehicle to protect his passengers from the rain. Júbilo lifted the canvas above his head with his hand in order to see the city. The wet streets heightened the beauty and charm of the capital, which was still quite small back then. In the east it extended to the San Lázaro train station, which is now the Cámara de Diputados, the House of Parliament. In the west it reached as far as the Río Consulado, to the Tlaxpana or what is known today as the Circuito Interior. To the north the boundary was the Alvarado Bridge, where the Buenavista train station used to be. And in the south the city ended at the Colonia train station, which is now Calle Sullivan. That was the whole city.

But it was more than enough to excite Júbilo, and to confirm for him that he was indeed going to be living far from the sea. The clacking of the carriage wheels as they glided over the cobblestones was a wonderful substitute for the familiar sound of waves. And as a welcoming gesture, the city presented him with its best sounds. To his delight, Júbilo discovered that the streets were filled with a cacophony of rustling, murmuring, screeching, a great buzz. And to top off the special afternoon, when he returned home he found Chucho, his new neighbor, waiting to initiate their new friendship by inviting him over to his house to listen to a radio program. A group of Chucho's friends from the *colonia* had gathered that day, the eighth of May 1923, to listen to the first concert ever to be transmitted by the radio station La Casa del Radio, which belonged to the newspaper *El Universal Ilustrado*. That night a whole new world opened before his eyes, or rather, before his ears. It seemed incredible to him that the voices of the announcers could be transformed into real presences, into true companions, which made his separation from friends, school, and family much less painful.

Eventually, his friendship with Chucho grew and they spent wonderful afternoons together listening to music after playing outside. They became inseparable, and Júbilo followed Chucho wherever he migrated, because Chucho's parents seemed to have a strange fascination for moving. They loved to change houses at the slightest provocation. Fortunately, they did so within the confines of the *colonia*, so it didn't interfere with Chucho and Júbilo's friendship. At most, they would have to get used to the new number of steps or blocks that separated one house from the other. But nothing ever managed to separate them or prevent them from getting together to listen to their radio programs.

As the years passed, the only thing that changed was the frequency with which they could get together. Júbilo entered school before Chucho and found himself immersed in a world of obligations and school-related tasks. Marbles, tops, balls, and other toys were relegated to the memory drawer. But he sought out his dear friend every weekend to go to the movies, to ride bikes, or to hide out and smoke. During the breaks from school, Júbilo always went to the Yucatán with his family. It was upon returning from one of these absences that he found Chucho had moved again. Júbilo was eager to visit him as soon as possible, because he wanted to show his friend his incipient mustache.

On his way to his friend's new house, Júbilo felt a knot in his stomach. It was the first time this had ever happened to him. He didn't know what to make of it. His stomach didn't really hurt, it just sort of trembled, as if wanting to tell him something. It was like a premonition, or fear. As he turned a corner, he caught sight of Chucho and waved at him: he was talking to two young people, a boy and a girl. As Júbilo drew nearer, his fear increased and he was tempted to turn and run away, but he couldn't do that because his friend had already seen him and, besides, the group seemed to be waiting for him. He suddenly remembered how one morning the pigeons that lived on the roof of his house had fled up into the sky: they had sensed the earthquake that shortly afterward shook the whole city. After taking the last few steps toward Chucho and his companions, he understood perfectly. Before him stood the most beautiful thirteen-year-old girl he had ever seen. Chucho introduced his new friends Luz María and Juan Lascuráin to Júbilo. When he reached out to shake hands with the girl, Júbilo nearly doubled over from the pain in his stomach. The touch of her skin transformed him completely and took away his ability to sleep from that moment on. With a smile, Luz María said she preferred to be called Lucha. Júbilo wanted to say something, but it suddenly became very difficult, and when he opened his mouth all that escaped was a sad squawk. They all laughed at Júbilo's changing voice and made him blush, but then he joined in their laughter.

The reason he laughed with them had nothing to do with the silliness of what had just happened: it stemmed from the enormous pleasure he felt in discovering a new sound. The sound of love. It was a murmur that sounded like laughter, like the breaking of waves, the crashing of happiness mixed with the music of dry leaves carried along by the wind, like sacred music vibrating in his stomach, in his hair, all over his skin, and, of course, in his ears. The sound of love stirred him up in such a way that for a moment he was left completely deaf. Still, Lucha responded. Charmed by his laughter, she invited him over to her house to listen to Glenn Miller's latest album. Júbilo eagerly accepted the invitation and they all headed for the Lascuráin home.

Lucha's house was the most popular meeting place in the *colonia*. The Lascuráins were a happy, generous, sharing family who always kept the door to their home open to others, and Júbilo was no exception. They immediately accepted him with open arms and adopted him into their circle. And he was deeply grateful, for several reasons. Because of the opportunity it gave him to make new friends. Because of the possibility of listening to the radio and the phonograph, equipment that didn't exist in his own home. And last, but most important, because of the chance to be near thirteen-year-old Lucha, the thought of whom kept him awake at night from that day forward. Lucha was two years younger than Júbilo, but as is quite usual, she was more developed than he was. While his voice was barely beginning to change and a ridiculous fuzz of a mustache was only just sprouting, Lucha already had a pair of fully developed breasts and appetizing hips that were growing more sensuous every day. Júbilo dreamed about her every night and without fail awoke with damp sheets. His best erotic fantasies featured her. His every ejaculation, from the first to the last, was dedicated to her. The whole world revolved around Lucha and because of her it had grown much clearer and brighter.

Shortly thereafter, Júbilo, who was in his second year of high school, learned in physics class that the Earth's magnetism is produced by the molten iron that spins around its nucleus. The professor had explained that an element called magnetite circulated in the bloodstream of both humans and animals, which allowed them to perceive the Earth's electromagnetic energy, but this enhanced perception was more pronounced in some individuals than in others. This explained why some animals could anticipate changes beneath the Earth's crust, as in the case of earthquakes, allowing them to flee, instead of waiting to be crushed to death. Júbilo immediately thought of the day he had first met Lucha. He was certain that his personal magnetite had been drawn into harmony with Lucha's magnetic center and had tried to prevent disaster. It had tried to warn him that his life was in danger, or at least the life he had led until then; that from that moment on, his story would be divided into before knowing Lucha and after, because their meeting had changed his life forever.

Júbilo believed that the iron circulating in Lucha's blood must be particularly special, because it managed to produce a magnetic pull as powerful as the earth's. The girl attracted men's desire as honey drew bees. And those unrequited desires kept spinning around her, increasing her natural magnetism to alarming levels. There was no boy in the *colonia* who didn't want to be her boyfriend, who didn't dream of giving her her first kiss, who didn't long to become one with her.

Júbilo turned out to be the lucky one. A few months after they met, during a Christmas *posada*, he declared his love for her, and to everyone's surprise, Lucha, the unconquerable, replied she loved him too. During the first months of their courtship, Júbilo was a most respectful *novio*. He did no more than just hold her hand and give her light kisses on the mouth. But gradually he dared to go further. Lucha remembered clearly the first time that Júbilo had inserted his tongue between her lips. It was a very strange sensation. She wasn't sure whether it had been agreeable or not. The only thing she knew was that the next day she couldn't look him in the eyes without blushing.

From there they moved on to long embraces, accompanied by similarly drawn-out kisses. With the passing of time, and as their trust built, not to mention their passion, they progressed to tighter embraces during which their bodies were pressed against one another . . . and, well . . . It reached the point where Lucha could distinctly feel the hardening of Júbilo's member pressing against her pelvis. After those embraces came the timid sliding of Júbilo's hand down Lucha's back. And that's where her problem really started. Lucha was accustomed to getting everything she wanted, but now that she was burning with desire for Júbilo to caress not only her back, but a little lower too, she had to repress the desire to ask him to. The same thing would happen when Júbilo held her hand as they sat in the *sala* listening to music. Sometimes, not wanting to, yet wanting to, Júbilo would brush his hand against Lucha's leg, and her skin would suddenly become covered with goose bumps. She was very aroused by the idea that Júbilo would openly caress her legs and that he might slide his hand up to her intimate parts, but the chance of that happening was curtailed by social convention. At any rate, for one reason or another, after Júbilo's visits, Lucha invariably ended up with damp panties, burning cheeks, and agitated breathing. Every day, they sought out with greater urgency opportunities to be alone together, but they weren't always successful. There was never a lack of busybodies to spy on them, whether it was one of Lucha's six unmarried siblings, her parents, or the servants.

However, one day the perfect opportunity presented itself. One of don Carlos's sisters had died and the whole family went to the funeral, except Lucha, who stayed home with a terrible headache. The origin of her illness was none other than the accumulated and repressed desire over the seven years of her relationship with Júbilo. While she was alone at home, Júbilo paid his regular visit.

They went into the *sala* and while they listened to a Glenn Miller record, Lucha took Júbilo's hand and placed it squarely on her breast. Júbilo's reaction, somewhere between surprise and satisfaction, was to accept the cordial invitation, and he caressed her breasts with impassioned tenderness. That day, Lucha knew that the time had come for them to marry, because it wasn't right for a señorita to permit her *novio* to caress her like that. And it wasn't until this moment that she had understood why! It was obvious that from here on there was no going back. Her passion was only going to grow stronger and she couldn't bear it any longer. She was tired of resisting the call of desire.

On the other hand, if she gave in now, it would be impossible for her to reach her wedding as a virgin, as her parents expected. To Lucha this social hypocrisy seemed totally absurd. If a woman's purity was shattered the instant she lost her virginity, that meant a man's penis was the most impure thing in the world. She couldn't agree with that. For many years, the nuns at school had been teaching her that God had made man in his own image. Therefore, there couldn't be a part of the human body that was impure, because each one was a divine creation. Besides, it seemed totally absurd to her to think that God had given men hands that weren't supposed to caress, and women clitorises that weren't meant to be touched. Of course, it never occurred to her to use this argument to convince her parents to let her marry Júbilo. But she used many others instead, until she managed to convince them that she was totally captivated by Júbilo and that it would be much better to allow her to marry him, in spite of the fact that at twenty-two he couldn't offer her a very promising future.

Lucha had gotten her way, but now that she had obtained what she had so desired, she realized a lot of other things were missing. She had never expected that being married would be so difficult, nor what it meant to be married to a poor man. Her parents had warned her, but who listens to parental advice when one is in love? No one. The time she spent in bed with Júbilo was wonderful, but then Júbilo would go to work and leave her alone. As soon as he closed the door, the house would grow silent. The laughter left with him. Lucha had no one to talk to. She missed her family. She missed her friends. She missed the bustle of her parents' house. She missed the shouts of the street vendors. She missed the whistle of the sweet potato vendor's cart. She missed the singing of the canaries at home. She missed her Victrola. She missed her records. If only she had a radio, she wouldn't feel so lonely. But she didn't have one. And she didn't see any possibility of acquiring one in the near future, since Júbilo saved every last centavo they had left over, in hopes of buying their own house some day.

A deep melancholy gradually overcame Lucha. There was no one with whom she could discuss her worries. The month they spent in each tiny pueblo didn't allow her enough time to establish the kind of friendship that would make her feel comfortable about confiding her problems. In addition, she found that the people in the provinces were very cliquey and gossipy. She didn't realize that her very appearance was enough to scandalize them. Her haircut and the way she dressed, which seemed copied from fashion magazines, never failed to raise whispers as she passed. Of course, people like to criticize anyone who appears different, so she was the perfect target. She was young, beautiful, dressed like a movie star, and drove her own automobile! How could she not attract attention? So Lucha felt isolated, and never more so than in Huichapan. The rain drove her into a deep gloom. She hated the absence of the sun. Her *mamá* had taught her as a young girl that the sun purified and bleached clothing. Lucha believed that its purifying power extended even further. She was convinced it also cleansed impurities of the soul. And in her house in Mexico City, well, her former house, her parents' house, she had always been able to go into the garden and lie in the sun when she needed to drive away sadness.

For a girl who grew up showered with indulgence and gratification, life with Júbilo was difficult to bear. Not because of any lack of love or attention from him, but because married life wasn't what she had expected. Lucha had imagined that, like her mother, she would have servants who would take care of all the household chores so she could dedicate herself to playing the piano, entertaining her friends, and shopping. Her parents had raised her to be a princess. She had attended a school for young ladies where she learned to speak English and

French. She knew how to play the piano, embroider, and set a proper table. She had taken courses in gourmet cooking. So she did know how to cook, but on a gas stove, not on coal. She excelled at French cooking, not Mexican. She didn't really know much about Mexico, and of its cuisine she knew even less. Her Mexico was limited to the capital, or rather, to the boundaries of her own *colonia*. She thought the people in every house in Mexico ate like they did in her parents' house and that all leftovers were stored in a refrigerator. She had never imagined that if she wanted a cup of coffee when she got up in the morning she would first have to light a fire in the stove. She didn't know how to. Nothing she had studied could help her. She was only now learning the things that no teacher had ever taught her: for starters, that food that is not refrigerated spoils, it rots and is invaded by bugs. It requires a very organized mind to survive without a refrigerator. To know what to buy, and how much. The refinements of her education didn't help her either when it came to washing laundry in the sink. She didn't have the slightest idea how to do it. At home, her mother had the latest-model wringer washing machine. Washing by hand required much more effort. And besides, she didn't have the right clothes for housework. She felt completely out of place, like a gringo on the dance floor.

The only good thing was that she could count on Júbilo's full support. At his side, all her problems vanished. The unknown Mexico appeared before her with a smiling face. In the company of her husband, food in the markets would taste delicious and even horse droppings would smell glorious. Thanks to Júbilo, Lucha was able to discover the real Mexico, provincial Mexico, the Mexico of the poor, the Indians, the forgotten. A Mexico that was gradually being covered by railway lines and telegraph poles, spreading out over its surface like a spiderweb. And Lucha couldn't help feeling like a fly about to be trapped by the spider, by some dark force hiding behind all this progress. She was unsettled by all the changes and by the other new developments she sensed were approaching. It all seemed so new to her: she felt insufficiently prepared.

Most of all, she resented the lack of money. If she only had money, everything would be easy. She would be able to buy herself a few dresses and shawls that would make her feel less out of place in the markets. The rough jute bags in which she carried her shopping had already ruined all her silk stockings. Her new life required new clothes, a new hairstyle, and new shoes, but she had no money. Nor did the person on whom she depended.

She had gotten married knowing that it was to a very young, very poor man, who had barely begun his career as a telegraph operator and who was not yet settled, but she had never imagined what all that really meant. All that had mattered to her was losing her virginity. Now she had to face the consequences, and forget her former life as a pampered young girl. She could no longer count on help from her mother, or her brothers, or her *nana*, nor on economic support from her father. Now she had to take care of things for herself. Light the fire in the morning, cook on coal, wash clothes by hand, dust, scrub, survive without perfume or Colgate toothpaste: and make sure that Júbilo didn't notice how dissatisfied she felt. He deserved more than that. He was very good to her and gave her everything he could. It wasn't much, but he gave it with true love. She had to admit that he struggled to make her happy, and while she was with him she never missed her *colonia*, her friends, her parties, her record player, or her radio. But when she was alone, she would cry when she counted the little money she had for the day's shopping. When she went to the market she had to count every last centavo and to make the coins stretch as far as she could. As she walked through the stalls she would count her money in her head and rack her brains to find a way to prepare a complete meal with the fewest ingredients. And once she had everything she needed, walking home she would go through all the options for cooking them, all the while dreaming of the day when economic hardship would disappear from her life.

The night Júbilo had won the bet with don Pedro, however, Lucha believed that moment had finally arrived and was immediately consumed by an obsession to spend all the money at once, but Júbilo prevented her from doing so, and this became the reason behind their first fight. Lucha lightly berated her husband, complaining that he never noticed all the things they had to do without, and Júbilo replied that he did indeed notice and that was precisely why they needed to save all the money they had. That way, they would sooner be able to buy a decent house as close as possible to Lucha's family, so she could stop missing her former life so much.

So one of them looked at a solution over the short term and the other, over the long term. One looked for a palliative for their problems and the other, permanent relief. Finally, after a long argument, they reached a compromise. Júbilo agreed to let Lucha buy a pair of slips and a shawl; and Lucha promised not to touch the rest of the money.

The opportunity to buy something new made Lucha very happy. One could even go so far as to say that the purchase of that shawl literally changed her life. She discovered an article of clothing that was truly not only useful but beautiful. From that moment forward, the shawl became an indispensable accessory to her attire. With her new shawl over her shoulders, Lucha walked tall. She felt like a different woman. It was the first time since getting married that she had shopped for clothes. She was so excited that on her way home, she stopped to buy some candles at another stand in the market. On the counter was a jar of chiles in vinegar, and another filled with olives. The smell of the olives filled the air. Lucha couldn't resist buying some: she had an irresistible urge to taste them. It had been months since she'd had an olive. And now, when the craving was so strong, was the time to buy them. She asked the merchant for 100 grams. But when she opened her purse to pay, she realized her money had evaporated. She had enough to pay for the candles, but not for the olives. Lucha fruitlessly tried to make up the difference by counting up the few centavos she had left in her purse, and in that instant don Pedro entered the store. He immediately understood the embarrassing situation in which Lucha found herself and, without thinking twice, extracted from his wallet the coins that were needed to complete the purchase, and put them on the counter, saying:

"Allow me, *por favor.*"

Lucha turned her head to confront a face full of evil, a face which, even when wearing its best smile, was unable to appear kind, and which belonged to none other than the man against whom her husband had won the bet. Lucha delicately, but firmly, refused the coins and replied:

"No. You are very kind, but there's no need for you to bother. I'll come back later and pay."

"A woman as beautiful as you doesn't deserve to be out walking in the rain. Please accept my humble assistance."

"Again, I thank you, but that is not necessary. It's no problem for me to go home and come back again, since I drove here, I didn't walk here in the rain."

"Well, at any rate, it doesn't seem right for you to have to make two trips. Please do not offend me, three centavos are not so important that they will rob anyone of sleep. Grant me the honor of helping you in some small way."

Don Pedro took Lucha's right hand and kissed it lightly, effectively ending the discussion. Lucha didn't know what to do. It was obvious this man had never accepted no for an answer, and since her craving for the olives had grown even stronger, she chose to say a hurried *gracias*, collect her purchases, and leave the stall with the feeling that she had just done something wrong. She had not liked at all the satisfied smile that appeared on don Pedro's face when she accepted his money. She didn't know to what to attribute it. She was unaware that don Pedro had just discovered Júbilo's Achilles' heel and now knew exactly where to attack him.

The olives didn't taste as good as Lucha had expected. Her stomach churned, twisted, and trembled. On the one hand, she felt the disagreeable sensation that she had just done something wrong. On the other, she felt enormous satisfaction at having allowed herself a small pleasure. It was a strange new feeling. Lucha didn't know how to assimilate what was going on inside her. She felt ashamed, as if she had somehow failed Júbilo. As if she had opened the door of her home to the devil himself. As if Júbilo and she were on the brink of danger, about to face something terrible and unknown. It was a premonition that unsettled and agitated her, provoking a nausea quite unlike anything she had experienced before. It reminded her of the way she had felt the day she met Júbilo, but this was quite different. On that earlier occasion the tickling in her stomach had been very agreeable. She had trembled, yes, but more from pleasure than from anything else. It had seemed like the response of a drum that someone has just struck. Her stomach had been shaken up for a while by the strong vibrations. But now the real

♣♣♣♣ LAURA ESQUIVEL

difference was that unlike the first time, when her stomach had been in tune with the loving energy Júbilo had sent her, this time she was responding to something hidden, dark, unknown, denied, but which was there, ready and waiting to shake her completely, to make her resonate with fury, to connect her with its black sun, with its dark light.

Lucha felt that this unknown energy had taken control of her soul. She couldn't get out of her mind the unpleasant sensation that don Pedro's lips had produced as they brushed against her hand. It made her sick just to think about it. That kiss had made her feel like a sinner. As if from that moment she had lost her innocence forever. As if she could never get back to who she had been. Trying to calm down, she went to the telegraph office. She wanted to hear Júbilo's healing laughter. She wanted to feel clean. She wanted to erase that disagreeable feeling and she could only do so in the company of her husband. When she was with him everything looked brighter.

Júbilo was delighted with her unexpected visit. The smile on his face made Lucha momentarily forget her worries. Júbilo's shining eyes instantly had the same effect on her as the sun's rays in which she used to luxuriate in the garden of her parents' house when she wanted to purify her soul. She felt like her old self again, clean, pure, light. Júbilo asked her to wait for a few minutes while he finished attending to a lady customer. It was close to lunchtime and he wanted to go home with her. Lucha agreed with pleasure and stepped away from the counter to allow her husband to work in peace.

The lady in question was a stallholder from the market who was going through the same thing Lucha had just suffered: she didn't have enough money to pay for the telegram she needed to send. Lucha's eyes filled with tears and she turned toward the street so Júbilo wouldn't notice. But it wasn't necessary, because her husband, with characteristic generosity, was so focused on solving the lady's problem that he had eyes only for what he was writing. He had suggested that she allow him to rewrite the message so that she could afford the cost of the telegram. The original telegram read: "I know that I owe you money and I have not been able to pay you. But however, I need ten boxes of tomato. I beg you to send them. As soon as I have sold them I will pay you for everything." After Júbilo's intervention, the message read like this: "I have made a good deal. With the sale of ten boxes of tomatoes, I can repay everything I owe you. Please send them urgently." The message was reduced by eighteen words and in the process Júbilo had not only corrected her grammar and spelling but also ensured that the humble woman really would receive the tomatoes.

The problem was that this gave Lucha time to be alone with her thoughts again and to dwell on what had happened at the market. She blamed it all on her lack of money. If she had had sufficient funds, she wouldn't have had to accept don Pedro's offer of help. Financial constraints caused all kind of embarrassments. Right now, this poor woman, with whom she completely identified, was suffering because of a lack of money, just as she had been at the market. She didn't like experiencing poverty, being exposed to it. It made her feel vulnerable and help-less. It terrified her to be dependent on a poor man. The world was made for the rich. Poor people had no oppor-tunities. Now she understood why the Mexican Revolu-tion had happened. Being poor was horrible. And if it hadn't been for accompanying Júbilo all over the country, she could never have imagined the conditions under which thousands of Mexicans were living. She knew Europe better than she knew her own country, and it hurt her now to discover its misery. Eating a bowl of soup at home takes money. Producing the fruits of the earth costs money. Traveling takes money. Building a house requires money. Installing telegraph lines takes money. Communicating with loved ones means money. And when a woman depends on someone else to get money, she can't make her own decisions. He who pays, rules. Those with money determine what, when, and how much a peasant eats. What kind of corn he plants. Even when the chickens should lay their eggs! It didn't seem fair to Lucha that one had to pay to send a telegram. That someone else could control contact between people; that only those who could pay for it could use a form of com-municating that should belong to everyone. All this was bothering Lucha, and many other things, because she wasn't accustomed to anyone telling her what to do with her life. The only thing that made her happy again was that Júbilo had just finished helping the stallholder and they could now go home.

Being close to Júbilo was an immediate comfort. By his side, all her problems disappeared, there were no insurmountable obstacles. Júblio had that gift. Lack of money immediately became unimportant. He didn't need cash to caress his wife's hand, to look into her eyes, to kiss her passionately, and to enjoy his erection. As soon as they got home they rushed into the bedroom to make wild love. Lucha was in the process of enjoying the way Júbilo's penis caressed her as never before, so she was greatly surprised when he brusquely separated from her.

"You feel different, Lucha. You're not the same."

Lucha's heart nearly stopped. She felt she had been found out. She didn't know how, but she suspected that Júbilo already knew that she had accepted three centavos from don Pedro. She averted her eyes so Júbilo wouldn't see her bewilderment, and she rapidly began to search for a believable excuse, but she only managed to stammer:

"Different? How?"

Júbilo didn't answer her. Instead he touched her belly with the palm of his hand and studied it. Suddenly he let out a loud laugh that filled the whole room.

"You're pregnant, *mi amor!* You're pregnant!"

He began to cover her with kisses. Lucha was stunned. It was true that her period was a week late, but since it was only such a short time she hadn't thought anything about it.

"How do you know?" she asked.

"I felt it. I can't explain it, but you have a different energy."

It was the first time Lucha had heard anything like that. She knew Júbilo had especially sensitive hands, but she couldn't imagine his powers extended that far. Yet she wanted to believe him. It wasn't that implausible. And once she thought about it a little, she decided in fact it was more than likely. Perhaps you could compare it to the way, by putting one hand on a patient's stomach and tapping gently on it with the other, a doctor can make a diagnosis from the way the sound echoes off the internal organs. It was possible that Júbilo could hear the way her womb echoed.

Lucha stopped doubting him, and immediately accepted that she was indeed pregnant. She had to believe it. That was the only explanation for the dizziness and nausea she had felt when don Pedro had kissed her hand. It was the only thing that made sense. And seen from that perspective, what she had done didn't seem so wrong. A pregnant woman's craving was sufficient excuse to salve her conscience. After all, if she hadn't satisfied that craving, she would have risked her baby being born with a face like an olive. With tears in her eyes, she hugged Júbilo and together they celebrated the wonderful news, unaware that fate had already chosen them as victims of misfortune.

Chapter 5

ON JÚBILO WOKE UP PANTING. For the last few days he had been having a recurring nightmare. He was diving at the bottom of the ocean, without an oxygen tank, but breathing as if he had one. His movements were slow and rhythmic. The water was warm and pleasant—a few brightly colored fish accompanied him as he swam. A soft light allowed him to see into the distance. Suddenly, he heard a murmur of voices, followed by laughter. The sounds were coming from the surface. Júbilo lifted his head and observed the bright sunlight filtering through the water, making it sparkle. At that moment, for no apparent reason, he recognized where he was. It was the place where he had first learned to swim. He recognized the waters as those that had washed over the beach in front of his parents' house so long ago. Júbilo was certain of it. And the laughter he heard in the distance belonged to his grandmother, Itzel; his mother, doña Jesusa; and his father, don Librado. Júbilo wanted to join the group to share in their laughter. He tried to swim ashore and get out of the water, but his feet were anchored in the sand. Try as he might he couldn't move them. Then he started to shout, but no one could hear him. The sounds that came out of his mouth were trapped in air bubbles, but when they reached the surface and burst, no sound was released. Júbilo was growing desperate. He shouted louder and louder, but things only got worse. Water began to enter his lungs, he began to drown, and nobody could help him. Fortunately, this time his daughter Lluvia had arrived to awaken him.

"*Papi,* your friends are here. What's the matter? Did you have a bad dream?"

Don Júbilo nodded his head. For a month now he had been practically unable to speak. He had to make enormous efforts for a few tentative sounds to issue from his mouth, but they were unfortunately totally incomprehensible to those who heard them.

Faced with this situation, Lluvia had immediately begun to search for a telegraph machine. The first place she went to had once been a telegraph office, but when she asked about a transmitter they nearly laughed at her. The telegraph transmitter, as such, had disappeared years ago and no one knew where she could find one. Then it occurred to her that perhaps she might be able to find one at Lagunilla, the flea market, but after several fruitless visits she gave up. She had no choice but to focus her search on antiques shops. She had to visit quite a few, both in the capital and in the provinces, before she found one at last.

When she finally had the telegraph transmitter she immediately wanted to show it to her father, but then she hesitated. She didn't want to do anything that might upset him. As soon as her father saw it, he would surely want to use it, and it might turn out to be very frustrating for him to send messages that no one could understand. Her children then informed her that a software program existed that allowed one to enter information into the computer via a telegraph transmitter, in Morse code, instead of through a regular keyboard. The computer would then "translate" the information from the telegraph into spoken words and display them on the monitor. That way everyone would be able to understand what her *papá* was "saying." Lluvia thought it was an amazing invention and she had immediately ordered a copy, but it would take nearly three weeks to arrive by mail. So as not to waste any time, she decided to learn to use the telegraph machine herself in the meantime, or at least to take a basic course that would allow her to understand without the computer the first words her father would "speak." The first person she asked for help was don Chucho, her father's childhood friend. But unfortunately he was unable to help, because his wife had had a stroke and had to be hospitalized.

Next she called Reyes, her father's old friend from work, to see if he could teach her Morse code. Aurorita, her father's nurse, was also eager to learn: she didn't want to be left behind. She had been don Júbilo's nurse long enough to have formed a solid, affectionate relationship with him. Over the years don Júbilo had become her close friend, her confidant, her adviser. Thanks to his wise advice Aurorita had learned how to handle the crises in her marriage better, to laugh at her problems, and to look at life positively. She was so grateful to don Júbilo that she would do anything she could to somehow repay the affection and support he had selflessly bestowed on her. So now Aurorita devoted the same attention and interest to Reyes's lessons in Morse code as she did to reading to don Júbilo, taking him out for strolls in his wheelchair, massaging his limbs, and feeding him.

The third member of the group of students was Natalia, the night nurse, whom everyone affectionately called Nati. She attended to don Júbilo during the night shift and just like Aurorita she had established a warm relationship with him. So much so that sometimes Lluvia was awakened in the middle of the night by the sound of laughter coming from her father's room, even though she slept with her door closed. Don Júbilo's jokes flew twenty-four hours a day, and Nati's fresh laugh celebrated them with unmatched enthusiasm. She was the best companion for his sleepless nights. She had a wonderful sense of humor and a truly unique capacity for tenderness. She was a short, round woman who had adopted don Júbilo just as if he were a small child: changing his diapers, giving him baths, and lulling him to sleep by softly singing his favorite boleros and maternally caressing his forehead.

Nati and Aurorita were important members of the trio of "don Júbilo's women" who now desperately missed his comforting words, his advice, and his stories. Don Júbilo's vocal cords, unbearably tense because of the medicines for his Parkinson's disease, had stiffened like steel bars that imprisoned his words inside him. So Lluvia, Nati, and Aurorita anxiously awaited the moment those words would be liberated from the prison that kept them knotted in his throat.

And so the telegraph machine appeared as the great savior, the great liberator, the great consolidator of hope and affection. And Lluvia, who for so long had resisted the use of technology, now could only bless it, since because of it her father would again be able to communicate with the world. But Lluvia's problem was that she didn't belong to the computer generation. Her children knew how to use the contraptions, but she didn't. She was fifty-one and a very active sportswoman. She didn't feel old at all. But when confronted with the world of computers, she discovered that she belonged to the old "on/off" generation, which only knew how to turn appliances on and off, and was light-years away from the computer skills of the younger generation. Her inability to handle the complicated machines created an unbridgeable generation gap. With difficulty, Lluvia had learned how to operate a VCR, and she did so in a very rudimentary fashion. She had no problem watching a movie on video, but she could not program the apparatus so it would automatically record a television program. And the operating instructions didn't help one bit. It seemed to her that in order to understand them, one needed a doctorate from Harvard. So whenever she bought a new electronic device, instead of unnecessarily complicating her life, she simply asked her children to show her how to operate it, and stored the instruction booklet in a drawer.

But now life had conspired to force her to try to understand how a computer functioned. And it was driving her crazy. She didn't understand anything. "Uploading" and "downloading" information seemed foolish to her. From where did one download it? And where was it uploaded to? Where was it stored? When one uploaded information through a portal, where did it go? Perla, her daughter, took on the task of explaining it all to her: that the Internet linked one to an international network of users and what "downloading" meant. That idea she did like. It was beautiful to feel that via the Internet one was connected to the whole world. The Internet, seen from Lluvia's inexperienced point of view, showed its most pleasant side, and appeared totally inoffensive. Of course, neither Perla nor Federico dared to tell their mother that, for example, the neo-Nazi movement was using it as a means to organize criminal acts and that with a few clicks anyone could obtain sufficient information to construct an atomic bomb. There was no real need. There were always going to be people who used technology toward humanitarian ends and others who chose the opposite. But why talk about that. Their mother already had enough to worry about, just learning how to use the computer and Morse code at the same time.

And if Lluvia was encountering difficulties, well, just think of poor Aurorita and Nati. They had never used a computer in their lives, and when they first put their hands on the keyboard they felt as strange as the first man on the moon must have. But their love for don Júbilo was enough to overcome any obstacles, and Lluvia was surprised by the learning ability the two humble women possessed. Perla had a lot of fun teaching them, but she believed they really didn't need to try so hard. All they really needed to learn was how to operate the computer. She saw learning Morse code as unnecessary. What was the point, if the computer was going to translate Morse code anyway? But don Júbilo's women argued, with reason, that they were doing it in case the computer malfunctioned or was down for some reason. They didn't want to have to depend on technology.

Their training was concentrated. They decided to meet in the evening, after Aurorita finished her shift. They waited for don Júbilo to eat dinner and fall asleep before they started class. Don Júbilo had a hospital bed with rails on the sides that served two purposes: to avoid accidental falls and to aid turning the patient over. From one of the rails, Lluvia hung the baby alarm that she used when her grandson slept at her house, allowing them to listen to any movement her father might make, although he usually slept soundly for about two hours, giving them time for their telegraph classes.

The lessons had the added benefit of a very pleasant musical background, because since his youth don Júbilo had grown accustomed to listening to the radio to fall asleep. His favorite station was 790 AM, which was devoted to nostalgic music. And so the best romantic boleros of all time would reach the adjoining room, which had been transformed into the Morse code classroom, via the radio lying next to don Júbilo's bed. This arrangement would create in Lluvia the conditioned reflex of listening to music while beginning to transmit messages.

In order to become a telegraph operator, one needed above all a good memory, since words were transmitted letter by letter and had to be memorized as they were received until a word was formed. Then the word had to be written down while one continued to listen to the rest of the message. It was a very strange and difficult thing to do, because of the delayed time frame, to always stay just behind the incoming message. Converting a signal into words was very difficult and tiring for the ears. A transmitting operator was said to have "good writing" when his messages were characterized by distinct, pronounced sounds, which made them easier to comprehend. But there were people who had terrible "writing" and used very loose sounds. This was the case for Lluvia, Aurorita, and Nati. The only one who had good writing was Reyes, but that was completely understandable; after all, he had been a telegraph operator for four decades. Despite not having transmitted for many years, he was able to get back up to speed in just a few hours. In contrast, don Júbilo's women were totally lost. They confused dots and dashes, mixed up sounds, or translated incorrectly. In short, they were a disaster, but they meant well.

In order to master the telegraph they were going to need many more hours, many more days, many more years, but in three weeks they had learned enough to understand don Júbilo's first words.

It was a memorable moment. Lluvia had asked Reyes and don Chucho to be present. She also invited Lolita, another close friend, who had spent her life working as a secretary in the Telegraph Office. Everyone arrived punctually. Already present in the house were Lluvia, her children Federico and Perla, and the nurses, Aurorita and Nati. Don Júbilo didn't suspect a thing until he learned that don Chucho was there. Then he guessed that something had to be going on for his friend to be there with him instead of at the hospital taking care of his wife. Of course, he never imagined the enormous surprise that awaited him. When his granddaughter Perla placed a portable computer and a telegraph transmitter on his legs, don Júbilo's face lit up. No one who witnessed that moment will ever forget the glorious smile that broke out on his face when his fingers felt the transmitter. There was no need to explain anything, he knew exactly why they had bought it and he didn't need any coaxing. Timidly, but firmly, he sent his first message. It was for his daughter Lluvia.

"*Gracias, hijita.* I love you very much," he tapped.

Lluvia's eyes filled with tears. To her father's surprise, she took the transmitter and responded in Morse code.

"Me too, *chiquito*," she answered.

Don Júbilo opened his eyes as wide as he could. His daughter knew Morse code! That was a surprise indeed. And it only got better when he found out that his other two women did too. Aurorita and Nati wanted their turn and each tapped out a message in Morse code that she loved him too. The unmistakable sound of the telegraph filled don Júbilo's room with joy. It was a very emotional moment. Lolita shed more tears than she had on that sad day in 1992 when Mexico's telegraph service died. She had been present at the ceremony at the Telegraph Office during which the telegraph was irrevocably retired as a means of communication. The telegraph operator who had the honor of transmitting the final message added, at his own initiative, "*Adiós*, my dear Morse, *adiós*."

Lolita had cried out of sadness on that occasion, but now she was crying with happiness. Tears had bid the telegraph farewell, now tears were welcoming it back. When Federico, who believed he knew his grandfather better than anyone else and who was aware that Júbilo didn't like to show his feelings in front of others, saw tears in the old man's eyes, he decided to interrupt the emotion of the moment with a short, but very precise, explanation of how the computer program worked. Federico and his grandfather had a great relationship. Lluvia's children were don Júbilo's favorite grandchildren, in contrast to his relationship with Raúl's three children, which was more distant. Raúl had moved abroad at a young age and only returned to Mexico with his children for vacations, and lately, not even then. The children were already married and had children of their own. Their lives were established outside the country, and they didn't visit their Mexican family as often as their relatives desired. Don Júbilo maintained contact with the other side of his family only through letters and telephone calls. On the other hand, he had been there when Lluvia's children were born, had helped them take their first steps, had played with them until they were all exhausted. He had taught them how to ride a bicycle, to spin tops and shoot marbles, and, since Lluvia's divorce, he had been like a second father to them: an understanding and loving father, who had guided them through adolescence, had taught them how to drive, had lent them his car when they needed it, and who never gave advice unless they asked for it, because he completely respected his grandchildren's individuality. Given this background, it wasn't hard to see why Perla and Federico adored their grandfather and were very upset by his illness.

Don Júbilo listened attentively to his grandson as he caressed the telegraph machine with trembling hands, as if it were the most precious object he'd ever possessed. When Federico finished his detailed explanation of the operation of the computer program, don Júbilo used the transmitter to speak.

"This opens up a world of possibilities for me. Thank you all very much."

"Thank you? What do you mean, *compadre?* We're planning to take advantage of your daughter's investment.

We're going to put you to work as a letter writer in the Plaza de Santo Domingo."

Don Júbilo let out a laugh such as Lluvia hadn't heard in a very long time.

"Did you know that your *papá*, sometimes, whenever he was really low on money—"

"Which means, all the time!" interrupted don Júbilo via telegraph.

"No, seriously, he worked in the Plaza de Santo Domingo for a while, writing love letters, and you can't imagine how successful he was at it . . ."

"Well, yes, but all jobs must end sometime. In those days I could see and speak and move around . . ."

"You can't see, but you sure do know what you're holding. Just look how you're handling that machine."

Everyone laughed and marveled that don Júbilo, despite not having used a telegraph transmitter in many years, could communicate without the least difficulty.

"*¡Qué bárbaro eres 'mano!* You're a great man! Not even I could handle the telegraph that easily," interjected his friend Reyes.

"What do you mean, 'not even I'? Do you think you're a better telegraph operator than I am?"

"Forget about him, Jubián! See how conceited he's become? It's because he takes less pills than the rest of us."

"That's not true, Chucho, you take less than I do."

"Me!? What's the matter with you!? I take pills for my high blood pressure, my digestion, my heart, and my asthma!"

"There you go! I take six pills. Two more than you."

"Don't fight, boys. As always, I've got you all beat."

"Very funny! With the life my Lucha gave you, anybody else would have had every illness in the book!"

"Maybe so, *chiquito*, but I chose her and put up with her, didn't I? There's some merit in that. If the two of you had looked for a woman as complicated, you would now both be beating me with your illnesses. . . ."

Lluvia, Perla, Federico, Aurorita, and Nati listened to their laughter, but didn't join in right away, because they couldn't yet follow the rhythm of telegraph communication. They had to wait for the message to appear in writing on the monitor before they could react. But despite the lag between their laughter and that of the others, they all enjoyed themselves equally. Lluvia was delighted to see her father "speaking," participating, captivating the others with his anecdotes again.

Through the computer, Lluvia learned about a joke that her father had played on Reyes years before, which had nearly given him a heart attack. For many years, they worked alone in a receiving office for Petróleos Mexicanos. Don Júbilo covered the day shift, and Reyes, the night shift. The job wasn't difficult, but it was very lonely. Júbilo missed his friends at the Telegraph Office. In the new position there was no one to talk to, or to tell stories. So he and Reyes established their own way to have fun. They would play jokes on each other. Practical jokes, silly jokes, innocent jokes, all kinds: the idea was to enjoy their work as much as possible.

In their office, they received messages from various oil wells. It was a large enough space to accommodate the enormous wireless receivers. But because the room was so big, it was very cold. The only people who occupied it were don Júbilo and Reyes. In the winter months, Reyes would use an electric heater, because the drop in temperature was unbearable for him. During the day, Júbilo had the advantage that the sun warmed the space a little; he could even sit outside in the sun at times, unlike Reyes. One night in December, in the middle of the *posada* season, Reyes arrived at work and turned on his heater as usual. He curled up in a chair to get warm. Shortly, he heard a series of loud explosions. He jumped out of his chair with his hair standing on end. His first thought was that the telegraph receivers had blown up. But when he went to investigate, he discovered that Júbilo had tied a package of firecrackers to the heater, and they had been set off when their fuses were ignited by the glowing heater. The following day, Reyes paid Júbilo back . . . and good. He simply called Lucha on the telephone and asked if she knew where Júbilo was, since he hadn't come to work in a week.

An eruption of laughter suspended all conversation around don Júbilo's bed for a few moments. Everyone knew how violent doña Lucha could get when she got mad and they could all imagine how it had gone for don Júbilo. When the laughter subsided a little, Lolita told them about one of the jokes that had been played at the Telegraph Office.

"Do you remember when they nailed Chuchito's desk drawer shut and he just kept pulling and pulling on it?"

"What about the time we rubbed carbon paper all over don Pedro's telephone?"

Unexpectedly, the laughter faded as don Júbilo grew serious. Lolita signaled with her hand for everyone to be quiet, and Reyes quickly changed the subject.

"*¡Sí, qué bárbaros!* I don't know how we dared, but the best was one day when Lolita had a huge pile of papers on her desk and I hid behind a nearby pillar. Then I took a fan and directed it at her without her seeing me. The papers flew off her desk and Lolita got up to chase them. She checked the window to make sure it was shut securely, and went back to her desk. Then I blew on her again . . ."

"*Sí, hombre,* don't go saying that you blew on her, because Lolita was always so proper."

Everyone laughed again except don Júbilo. Lluvia noticed this. Something had happened. Her father's good mood had vanished.

"Who was this don Pedro, Lolita?" Lluvia asked her father's friend as she walked her to the door.

"A guy that your father never liked, that is, really, none of us liked him. Well, darling, I must leave, because it's late."

Lolita was usually very talkative and she always stood at the door to chat for a while before she left. In fact, it was usually difficult to get her to stop talking, so the fact that she had left in such a hurry left Lluvia even more intrigued than she already was. If Lolita didn't want to talk about don Pedro, it meant something fishy had happened. Lluvia was dying to find out what it was, but it would have to wait for another day, because now, more than anything, she desperately needed to relax in a hot bath. It had been a day of intense emotions.

Water, her favorite element, exercised a magical power over Lluvia. It relaxed her instantly. Floating like a corpse, she was usually able to reach a deep calm in seconds, but this time she couldn't. She tried to concentrate on the look of happiness on her father's face when he had accepted the telegraph machine, but her mind kept drifting back to his serious, sad look after don Pedro's name was mentioned. A look she had never seen for herself until now: it had left her very unsettled. That afternoon, she had glimpsed that same look in a photograph that Lolita had brought as a gift for her father. It was an old photograph. From the group of telegraph workers, Lluvia could pick out Lolita, without the glasses she now wore, as well as don Chucho with hair, Reyes without gray hair or a belly, her father in perfect use of all his faculties, and her mother proudly displaying her pregnancy. It was a quiet photograph. Somber.

The group seemed to be celebrating a birthday or similar occasion, but from the sad expression on her father's face, she could tell he was not at all happy. Something was troubling him, causing him pain. Next to him stood her mother, beautiful, as always. Her father was holding her around the waist, but despite their physical closeness, Lluvia perceived an abyss between them. On the back of the photo was the date it had been taken, September 1946. Two years before she was born.

She figured her mother was about five or six months pregnant in the photograph. As she was about to use her fingers to count the months and calculate the due date, Lluvia realized that all this time she had been unconsciously tapping the fingers of her hand, as if she were sending telegraphic signals. She was thrilled to find that her hands practiced automatically. If she kept this up, in no time at all she would be as swift as her father at transmitting messages. She was distracted for an instant, concentrating on her hands and reflecting on the movement her busy fingers were making in the bathwater. She was particularly intrigued when she noticed that the more movements she made, the more waves were generated. She concluded that the number of times that something happened was very significant.

For example, one kiss was not the same as a thousand, nor one orgasm the same as five. The ether vibrated in a different manner, depending on how often an event had been repeated. This led her to think that numbers not only represented sums of money, as was her *mamá's* thinking, but had a much more profound significance, because they had a direct relationship to the cosmos. Whenever one used a number, one was subject to it. Numbers were like archetypes. She found the same occurred with words. Each one had a different resonance and therefore had a different echo in the ether. Then she came up with the idea that there must be an intimate relationship between numbers and words. They must have a connection similar to that between the buttons on a remote control and a television signal, and Lluvia wanted to learn what it was. She began her search that very instant. As a first step, she used her fingers to "write" a word in Morse code. She used her fingertips for the dots, and the length of her fingers for the dashes. In this way she carried out a conversation with herself in dots and dashes. Next, she converted the dots and dashes into corresponding numbers in Mayan numerology, and tried to work out their meaning. Finally, she realized that she had chosen the names of her father and mother, and that the sum corresponded to the month of September 1946.

This discovery drew her thoughts back to the photograph. Using her fingers again, she counted the months remaining before her mother would give birth: she realized that it would have been far later than the date Raúl was born. She had never been told of the existence of another sibling besides Raúl. What had happened? She knew she couldn't ask her father that kind of question given his present state of health, so her only other alternative was to make a visit to Luz María Lascuráin, to doña Lucha.

Chapter 6

PART FROM LOVE, there is nothing more important than confidence, and the opportunity to enjoy it is one of the benefits that married life offers. The confidence to bare one's soul, to expose one's body before the eyes of one's companion without the slightest trepidation, to give oneself freely, to open oneself, to abandon oneself shamelessly to another's arms without fear of being hurt. The confidence to be able to say to one's husband or wife, "Darling, you have a piece of spinach in your teeth," or, from another perspective, to be informed that one has snot hanging from one's nose.

Love and confidence go hand in hand. Only confidence allows loving energy to flow and insures intimacy between two human beings. The first sign that confidence no longer exists between two people is when one of the parties resists personal contact, when he or she is noticeably unwilling to receive caresses, kisses, hugs.

During the eight years that Lucha and Júbilo had been married, they had reveled in their confidence in each other. Neither had ever hurt the other, or had given any cause for suspicion. They loved and respected each other despite the huge differences between them. Without a doubt, the most revealing difference had to do with Lucha's dissatisfaction with the life that Júbilo offered her. What's more, Júbilo was convinced that this was the reason his wife had not been able to get pregnant again, something that, truthfully, didn't worry him terribly. Not because he didn't want to have more children, but because his salary as a telegraph operator was barely enough to provide for Lucha and Raúl, his firstborn. For the time being he couldn't afford the luxury of feeding more children. Well, at least not in the way Lucha expected. She demanded a lifestyle that Júbilo was very far from being able to provide.

With the money he had won in the bet with don Pedro, after deducting the amount he had given Jesús and Lupita for their wedding, he had somehow come up with enough for a down payment on a house that was acceptable to his wife. It was small, but comfortable enough and located as close as possible to his in-laws' residence. It was just inside the *colonia* Santa María la Rivera, but on the edge bordering on Santo Tomás. The house wasn't as large as the Lascuráins', but it was very pleasant. It had an elegant *sala* with balconies facing the street, three bedrooms with high ceilings and wooden beams that opened onto a tiled corridor at the end of which were a dining room and a bathroom. Next to the dining room was a large kitchen and a back patio where Raúl could play all he liked.

For a while Lucha felt very happy. The opportunity to settle in the capital and leave behind the nomadic life they had lived until then was more than enough for her. Arranging their scant pieces of furniture was as much fun for her as playing house. She thoroughly enjoyed everything that had to do with setting up their new home. For the first time in their marriage, she felt free to hammer a nail into a wall or to put a vase of flowers anywhere she chose. The houses and hotels where they had previously lived were temporary places that had never belonged to them. And for Lucha it was important to own things before she could enjoy them.

Júbilo, on the other hand, was able to claim the whole world with just a look. He could enjoy the scent of the gardenias without caring whether they came from the neighbor's garden or a pot on his own patio. He knew how to take the pain and misfortune of others and make it his own. He knew how to share his friends' dreams and to celebrate as his own the triumphs of those around him. Perhaps this was the reason he was so successful as a telegraph operator. When he sent a message, he did it with his entire soul, as if acting on his own behalf. And maybe it was for this same reason that he longed for direct contact with the public. In the tiny pueblos where he served as a telegraph operator, he was able to follow the result of the missives he sent, because he saw immediate replies to many of the telegrams, but in the capital his work turned cold, it lost its human warmth. He never found out what happened after the telegrams were sent, and as a result he was less satisfied by his work, it lost some of its meaning. He no longer knew why he worked so hard. His work as a mediator, as someone who brought others together, turned into a job in a large office where he had to send and receive messages as fast as possible, and where speed was valued above efficiency. Júbilo felt somewhat let down, but on the other hand, he knew he was doing the right thing, what Lucha expected from him, what his child needed. He worked for them, not for himself, and that brought its own pleasures. The satisfaction of seeing Lucha set up in her own house and of being able to feed and clothe his child adequately made him very happy.

Lucha appreciated his efforts, but still the money she received from him wasn't as much as she expected, especially now that they had a child to care for. She wanted to give Raúl the best education, buy him the best shoes, the best bicycle, the best ball. She felt hampered by the lack of money, so for several years she had been pressuring Júbilo to take on a double shift, and she constantly criticized his lack of ambition. To Júbilo her criticism seemed unjust. It wasn't that he had no goals in life, they just weren't the same as the ones Lucha embraced. He wasn't in a hurry to get rich, that wasn't his greatest aspiration in life. Jesusa, his mother, had always told him that wealthy people were so poor that they only had money. He agreed with that completely. There were more important things in life than the simple accumulation of capital. To him, a rich man was a man who had the capacity to be happy, and that's what he tried to be.

When Raúl was born, Júbilo was barely twenty-two, and Lucha was twenty. They were still very young. They had married so young that Júbilo hadn't had time to have fun with his friends. The first few months after his first child was born, Júbilo was completely off balance. He saw Raúl as an intruder who came to take away Lucha's love and attention from him. But as soon as the child began to smile and interact with him, his feelings for his son changed completely. He began to see in Raúl the younger brother he'd never had, and the child soon became his playmate. They developed such a close relationship that when Raúl began to speak, his first word was *papá*, and when he got hurt, instead of crying and shouting for his mother, he called out for his father. A father who was too young, who seemed more like a big kid himself, and who after a long day of work at the Telegraph Office only wanted to relax, play a little with his son, and then meet his friends to play the guitar and sing.

But for Lucha, this indicated his total lack of interest in advancing in life. She felt that Júbilo, instead of wasting his time with *"la guitarrita,"* should be taking English classes, or French, or accounting, or looking for a better job, anything that would assure her and her son of a more promising future. Because he who only looks at the short term is not well rewarded, shall we say. Raúl was growing up and she wanted to send him to a good private school, like Colegio Williams or somewhere similar. Júbilo didn't think that was necessary. When he had first arrived in the capital, his father had enrolled him in that very school.

But he had been able to attend the school for only a short time because the family's savings quickly ran out, and they had no choice but to move him to a public school. In fact, Júbilo had been much happier at the public school than he been at Colegio Williams, and he didn't see any reason why his son wouldn't feel the same. Lucha, in contrast, had attended the Colegio Francés and she was appreciative of it. She thought receiving a good education was a basic necessity. She never said as much to Júbilo, but she thought the difference between the two of them, in terms of education, was very noticeable. Júbilo didn't speak English or French, he knew nothing about Europe, he didn't know how to get ahead in society; therefore, she thought, he was condemned to a mediocre life. Lucha, on the other hand, believed she was capable of finding a good job any time she pleased. Every now and then in their discussions, she would propose this possibility, but Júbilo always rejected it immediately. He didn't think it was at all proper for his wife to work. He had been raised to be the sole provider for his family.

So, in order to avoid further arguments about money, Júbilo gave in. He put aside his evenings of playing with Raúl, the trio he was forming with his friends, the songs of Guty Cárdenas, his dreams of singing on XEW, and took a second job as a radio operator for the Compañía Mexicana de Aviación, where he worked after his shift at the Telegraph Office.

Thanks to the second job, in a short time they were able to buy a new refrigerator, a wringer washing machine, and an electric water heater to replace the wood-burning one. Lucha was content and that made Júbilo happy. For a while, family life improved noticeably. Lucha had time to go for walks, to go to the beauty salon, and to go shopping, since the washing machine, her electric skillet, and her blender saved her a great deal of time. She was very grateful to Júbilo for having bought her these things that were so necessary, and she never tired of praising the merits of the refrigerator and the other domestic appliances. Júbilo barely heard her, since he arrived home dead tired and had to struggle before falling fast asleep to listen to the detailed story of everything his wife had done that day.

Then Lucha found a new reason to argue with her husband: she criticized his lack of interest in her conversation, and his failure to notice that she had had a manicure and pedicure in his honor. Júbilo lovingly and patiently explained that he wasn't being inattentive, but that for him it was much more important to use the brief moments they had together to make love to her, instead of wasting his time and energy on idle chat. Lucha became furious and told him she needed someone she could talk to, not just someone to screw: she wasn't a prostitute. Júbilo ran out of arguments. For him it was much more rewarding to demonstrate to his wife that she still drove him crazy, and he just couldn't understand why it was more important to Lucha that he sit down to listen to her and look at her.

Fortunately, these arguments usually didn't last long. Their first embrace would lead to kisses, hugs, apologies, and forgiveness; and they would end up intertwined in bed.

It was after one of these reconciliations that Lucha went on the attack again and begged him to let her go out to work. Júbilo, tired of refusing her and finding it harder every day to buy everything Lucha wanted, granted his wife's request on the one condition that she look for work at the Telegraph Office. He felt that if they were both going to be working, they should at least find a way to be together a good part of the day.

Lucha's parents, in spite of their total disapproval of their daughter's desire to seek work because no woman in the family had ever done so before, decided to help her. Thanks to their influence, they were able to get an appointment with the director of communications, and asked him to give Lucha a job as private secretary to the director of the Telegraph Office. Even though she hadn't studied to become a bilingual secretary, she spoke perfect English and French. Lucha got the job, not so much because of her command of the two languages but because of her beauty. The director of the Telegraph Office thought that having such a good-looking secretary would elevate his status.

In fact, Lucha's presence in the office elevated not only the director's status but the whole institution's. Júbilo never became jealous; on the contrary, he felt extremely proud of the fact that this woman who aroused such admiration and desire in others was his wife. Of course, most of his colleagues were his closest friends, and, much as they admired Lucha, no truly sinful thoughts ever crossed their minds. Júbilo could see this in their eyes, so he never saw the least danger in Lucha's passing among the desks to everyone's obvious delight, because he was the principal beneficiary. Having his wife in the office was the best thing that could have happened to him. With her at his side, everything glowed. Júbilo and Lucha spent their happiest years there in the Telegraph Office. Sharing a common daily schedule allowed them to maintain their loving relationship. They would gaze lovingly at each other as they passed in the corridors; they looked for one another constantly and took advantage of even the briefest opportunity to give the other a kiss, caress a hand, or exchange a hug. When they were alone together in the elevator, they would kiss and embrace passionately. Sometimes they even went to the extreme of locking themselves in the bathroom to make love. They were more like lovers than spouses, and it was difficult to imagine them as the parents of an eight-year-old boy.

Looked after by his grandparents, Raúl grew and developed rapidly, and although at first he missed his parents, it wasn't difficult for him to get used to living surrounded by toys and his grandparents' loving attention from Monday to Friday, then spending the weekends with his parents. Saturdays and Sundays were like holidays for the Chi family. Júbilo somehow managed to counteract the strong influence that Raúl's grandparents had on the boy. Júbilo took his son to the markets to eat, to the floating gardens at Xochimilco, he showed him the most interesting corners of the capital so he would have a broader vision of what Mexico really was. He felt it was vital for his son to know his traditions and his cultural heritage before he was exposed to other cultures.

Lucha would use Júbilo and Raúl's outings to rest, to lie in the sun on the back patio, and to recover her strength before returning to work on Monday morning. The weekends were often spent in pajamas and a robe, except for the weekends when Raúl went to stay with his grandparents at their house in Cuernavaca, which were spent in bed, totally naked.

Lucha's working helped the young couple enjoy several years of renewed passion. With money in her purse for stockings and dresses, she recovered her joy for life and it seemed as if all of her problems had vanished. However, fate was soon to interrupt their lives in an untimely manner and turn them upside down.

The first sign of the change was the news of Lucha's new pregnancy, which took them by complete surprise. Neither of them had expected it. They had convinced themselves that Lucha had become sterile after Raúl's birth. Now, to their dismay, they realized this was not the case. It is also worth mentioning here that this news coincided with the return into their lives of a character they thought was long forgotten: don Pedro, the cacique from Huichapan.

Don Pedro belonged to a group of opportunists who took advantage of the Mexican Revolution to place themselves in government posts, where they stole everything they could lay their hands on. Shortly after Júbilo won the bet against him in Huichapan, don Pedro joined the PRI, the Institutional Revolutionary Party, and arranged to be appointed as a national representative in congress. Later he went on to occupy various administrative posts, among which director of the Telegraph Office was the least important, but he wasn't about to complain, he knew he had to show his obedience and loyalty to the party. A person like him, addicted to power, would even be willing to accept the position of a bathroom inspector in a bordello, just to remain inside the inner circle. Besides, from what he saw during his first tour, it wasn't going to be bad at all. The first thing that caught his attention about the Telegraph Office wasn't the antiquity or the architecture of the beautiful building, but the ass of the woman who was to be his private secretary, so shapely and, although he didn't know why, so familiar.

"Haven't we met before?" he asked her directly when she was introduced to him.

"*Sí*, señor, we met when my husband was working briefly in Huichapan as a telegraph operator, several years ago now," Lucha responded.

"Of course! How could I forget that? Your husband won a very memorable bet against me. . . . Well, well, isn't life interesting, I've just arrived and already I have old acquaintances in the office."

The news lay heavier than rotten fish on Júbilo's stomach. Having such a hateful person as his boss didn't please him one bit. When they greeted one another they did so coldly, as befits old adversaries. It was obvious that don Pedro was not at all happy either to have the husband of the secretary he'd already been eyeing working under his command. And he was a man whose actions followed his eyes. Only this time it was going to be a little more difficult. The look in Júbilo's eyes told him that. Curiously, don Pedro would never have recognized his old poker opponent if he hadn't remembered his wife's ass. Júbilo had grown a full mustache, which made him look much more handsome and manly. It was don Pedro who hadn't changed at all. The only thing he had added to was his belly, but the rest was exactly the same. He was still the same unscrupulous man, only now he had more influence and had learned better tricks. Júbilo knew perfectly well what the man was capable of and soon his suspicions were confirmed. When don Pedro took over, he did so completely. He acted as if the whole institution belonged to him—the building, the desks, the telegraph machines, the telegraph operators . . . and the secretaries—as if he could do whatever he wanted with them, as if he could take, manipulate, and use everyone in any way he wished. Soon rumors began to spread about how he went too far with the secretaries.

Obviously, his primary target was Lucha. She was the

one he fancied the most and also the one who worked closest to him. Going to work became a torment for Lucha. Not only was she going through the first months of her pregnancy with its accompanying nausea and vomiting, but she had to put up with don Pedro's insinuations. She constantly felt his gaze on her breasts or her rear. Lucha didn't know how to hide them any more. And to make matters worse, they were growing bigger every day because of her pregnancy. Which don Pedro didn't seem to notice, the pregnancy that is, not her voluptuousness, of that he was acutely aware, regardless of the fact that Lucha was happily married. What's more, her condition seemed to excite him. His attacks grew more vigorous every day. At first he had limited himself to brushing up against her, but gradually don Pedro began to rub her shoulders when she was sitting at her desk as he paced behind her. Flowers and chocolates started to appear on her desk with little notes, and finally he started baiting her with words. Sometimes after dictating a letter he would try to talk to her.

"What's wrong, Luchita, do you feel sick?"

"No, señor."

"Well, you seem so serious with me."

"No, it's not that, I just feel a bit under the weather."

"You see? Then you do feel sick. I really don't know how that husband of yours can make a beautiful woman like you work."

"He doesn't make me work. It was a personal decision."

"Well, if it was your own decision, it must have been forced by circumstances. No woman leaves her home and her children for pleasure. . . . Tell me, wouldn't you rather be at home right now surrounded by comfort and lots of trinkets, instead of hanging around here listening to an old flirt like me?"

Lucha had to think very carefully before she answered. If she agreed, don Pedro would take it as confirmation that she was forced to work by her circumstances, but if she said no, he might misinterpret it to mean that she loved to be in that office listening to an old man who, beyond being a flirt, was totally immoral. So Lucha simply shrugged her shoulders and left his office.

But when she got back to her desk, her boss's powerful words began to have an effect on her. She felt angry at Júbilo. Of course she would love to be at home enjoying her pregnancy and feeling clean and pure, instead of having to protect her belly from don Pedro's obscene ogling. Those thoughts intensified her nausea, causing her to throw up in the ladies' room.

Júbilo, in turn, was also annoyed. The office was no longer a safe place for them. There was constant danger in the air and he didn't know what to do. He felt totally impotent. He was doing everything he could to support his family with dignity. He already held down two jobs. If only there were thirty-six hours in a day instead of twenty-four he could find another. He was desperate to get his wife out of the office, but Lucha wouldn't let him. At first she had been tempted to quit, but Júbilo and she had plans to buy a new house that was a little larger, with an extra bedroom for the new baby, and they needed her salary for that. So she decided to keep her job and stay as far away from don Pedro as possible. But that only made Júbilo angry at her, and it also made him less efficient at work, because he was constantly alert to what was going on between Lucha and don Pedro.

JÚBILO WASN'T THE ONLY one who was worried. Uncertainty took hold of the office and drastically changed the personal and work relationships that had existed before don Pedro had arrived. Layoffs didn't take long to occur and everyone feared for his head. The confidence that had reigned before began to disappear. The jokes and laughter faded away. Nobody felt free or confident enough to indulge in them anymore. The only one who could have changed the situation was Júbilo, but he was too preoccupied with his own concerns. The atmosphere grew worse day by day, hour by hour, until it reached a climax. Lucha was seven months pregnant and was taking a break with Lolita. Lucha's unborn baby also decided to take advantage of the rest period by moving and stretching in her belly. Lolita was fascinated by the new shape of Lucha's belly and, full of curiosity, she asked Lucha if she could feel the child's movements. Lolita was an unmarried woman who had spent most of her life working in that office, and she was dying to rub the stomach of a pregnant woman. Of course, Lucha granted her dear friend's request, and they were lost in their own world when don Pedro appeared and asked Lucha if he too could touch her stomach. He used the same reasons as Lolita, that he was very curious about feeling the unborn baby's movements.

Lucha was torn: she had no desire for this man to touch her, but she couldn't think of a reason for denying him. If she refused him, she would seem rude since she was already allowing Lolita to touch her stomach. While Lucha ruminated on these thoughts, don Pedro took matters into his own hands. He removed Lolita's hand and put his in its place. As he did so, he took advantage of the opportunity to brush Lucha's breast. Lucha didn't even have time to get angry, because at that very instant Júbilo arrived in a fury and forcefully tore don Pedro's hand away.

"I don't want you to ever put your hand on my wife again," declared Júbilo.

"You are not in a position to give me orders," retorted don Pedro.

To which Júbilo responded by punching don Pedro squarely in the face. It was a powerful right hook, worthy of Kid Azteca. As don Pedro's heavy body rolled down the stairs that Júbilo had only moments before hurriedly climbed, a dense silence hung in the air. No one could believe what had just happened. The friendly, the jovial, the attentive Júbilo, a friend to all, was picking a fight, and with none other than the boss, the hated and feared enemy of all. It goes without saying that everyone sided with Júbilo, but they had to hide the fact, as they held their breath. Reyes tried to help his boss rise from the floor, but his offer was refused.

"Nothing happened. I just slipped. Get back to work!"

Don Pedro stood up, shook off the dust, removed his handkerchief from his pocket to stanch the blood dripping from his mouth, and headed for his office. As soon as he closed the door behind him he began to plot his revenge. He had always been a poor loser and this was the second time Júbilo had defeated him. What bothered him most was that he had been made to look foolish. He could never forgive that. His injured mouth hurt, but not nearly as much as his wounded pride.

Júbilo had just signed his death warrant in the office, but he didn't care. He felt he had done the right thing. All that remained now was to convince Lucha to submit her resignation along with his. But Lucha felt that it was better to calm down and to think things through clearly. They were in no position to be unemployed, especially if it was to be both of them.

For this and other reasons, the surprise birthday party they had organized for Lolita was ruined. They had planned to present her with a cake and sing the customary birthday song. The party didn't turn out to be as much fun as previous occasions. Everyone missed Júbilo's jokes and laughter. Neither he nor anyone else in the office was in a mood for joking that day. For there to be laughter, an atmosphere of confidence is necessary, and this was rapidly dwindling away in the Telegraph Office. Reyes struggled more than ever to enliven the gathering, but the most he was able to do was raise a chuckle from his fellow workers. Nevertheless, it was enough to provide an opportunity for a photograph to be taken.

LLUVIA LOOKED AT THE photograph carefully. She had no doubt that her mother was pregnant. The signs were obvious. She noticed that her mother had her hands on her belly as if trying to protect the creature within from some imminent danger. She turned the photo over and confirmed that it had been taken in 1946. Two years before Lluvia had been born. There must be some mistake. The photograph suggested that her mother had gone through a third pregnancy. It wasn't possible. It seemed strange that for so many years no one would have mentioned it, especially her mother. Doña Luz María Lascuráin didn't lie. Lying was one of the most condemned forms of behavior in their home. It was shocking to discover that her mother had broken the moral code by which the family had always lived. But after a little thought, she decided that perhaps her mother hadn't lied so much as hidden information.

And her father? What was his reason for keeping quiet? Why would he keep the birth of his child a secret? Maybe the pregnancy hadn't reached term and the birth in question had never occurred. In any case, there was no justification for their having hidden it this way. And what about Raúl? He had been eight at the time, and that wasn't so little. If another child had been born, Raúl would surely remember it. But what if he didn't? What if he, like she herself, knew nothing about it? But then she thought to herself it was most likely that Raúl did know about it and had not said anything because of his overprotective nature. That attitude of her brother's had always bothered Lluvia. He thought of her as a weak, helpless child that he had to take care of, as if she were incapable of defending herself. Lluvia was tired of still being treated like the baby sister. Why had everyone conspired to hide this information from her? More than deceived and betrayed, she felt angry.

Chapter 7

I WONDER HOW MUCH time passed between the moment God said "Let there be light" and the appearance of light? Sometimes, the mere difference of a single second between one event and another can be enough to turn our lives around one hundred and eighty degrees.

When does love turn into hate? How is that point reached? What unleashes such a transformation? Do there have to be continuously repeated insults or assaults, or can just one isolated incident be destructive enough to end a loving relationship?

In architecture, houses can crumble away little by little over the course of years; or they can be demolished in the blink of an eye by a powerful explosion. Cities and neighborhoods can be gradually transformed by time; or they can be devastated in an instant, in the few seconds that an earthquake lasts. A human being can go into a slow decline; or an unexpected bullet can erase him from the world in an instant.

Similarly, deep inside us, the opinion we have of a person can grow over the years; or it can decline in a flash. Words of encouragement can bolster our own self-confidence; or wounding or insulting words can destroy it. And others close to us can make us better people; or they can continually erode our self-esteem. Sometimes a single word, just one, is enough to wipe out years of psychoanalysis. So, each time I go to visit my mother, I have developed the habit of preparing myself by building up barriers to protect me from her negative words, her resentment, and her distrust.

"*Hola, m'hijita, ¿cómo estás?*"

"*Bien, mamita, ¿y tú?*"

"I'm okay, I suppose, you know I'm never free from suffering, but let's not talk about me. Let me look at you. It's been so long since you've come to see me. . . . *Ay m'hijita*, just look how skinny you are! I've told you before, I don't want you killing yourself taking care of your father. What you need is a rest, go to the beach, sit in the sun. If I were you, I would check him into a place where they would take good care of him, then at least you could live a normal life. You look worn out, exhausted, and I'm sure it must be hard for your children to have so many people in the house. It's not fair. . . ."

"It's not fair to send *papá* to an institution either. I've already told you . . ."

"Okay, okay, let's not argue. I won't meddle in your life. I'm just telling you what I think. . . . Oh, and by the way, how is Perla?"

"Fine, *mamita*, she's got her *novio* . . ."

"*Ay, m'hijita*, that really worries me! You're so distracted by your *papá* you're not even aware of the huge problem you're facing there. If your daughter gets all hot and bothered and ends up making the wrong decision, her tears will never stop! You really ought to talk to her. I don't like it at all. They've been *novios* for so many years, and they're still not married. Look, at the last party where we were all together, I don't know if you noticed, but they didn't care one bit that all the rest of us were around. They just went on holding hands and kissing each other and, *mira, m'hijita*, let me tell you, when *novios* don't care about others seeing them, well, you'd better watch out!"

"*Ay, mamá*, leave them alone. Let them live their own lives."

"No, I'm not going to butt in, I already told you, I'm not going to interfere in anybody's life."

"Good!"

"What I will say is that I'm very worried, because men, all of them, listen to me now, never think about anything except filth, they're all a bunch of pigs. . . ."

IT'S TIME TO REINFORCE the walls, to brick myself in, to raise the protective barriers! I knew by heart the speech that was to follow: *Men! They're all the same. They don't think about anything except screwing anyone who happens to go near them, whether it's a neighbor, a servant, or their son's wife. Men are disgusting pigs who feed on garbage and will even screw a rat. . . .* I don't know what men my mother is talking about. As far as I know she only had one boyfriend, and she married him. And as hard as I try, I can't remember a single shred of my father's personality that could fit her description. On the contrary, I remember him washing dishes, standing in line to buy fresh tortillas, stuck in the kitchen on Sundays preparing *cochinita pibil*, that delicious roast pork from his native Yucatán, and all the while watching over Raúl and me. I never caught him casting a libidinous glance at a neighbor or a servant or anyone else. If he ever did, he took care to do it far from home. But I am not going to argue with my mother. Rather than make any comment, I prefer to raise my eyebrows, which can be interpreted in a thousand different ways, and to change the subject to avoid further argument.

"*Oye, mamita,* how is Raúl?"

"*Bien.* I spoke with him yesterday on the phone and he asked me about your *papá.* I told him that your father is very sick and he agrees that you should put him in a home."

"Instead of giving you his opinion, he should call *papá* more often."

"What are you talking about?! You know how busy he is. And you, instead of speaking ill of your brother, you should thank him for sending you money to pay for the nurses. If it weren't for that, just imagine what a disaster it would be! That's why I say you should . . ."

"*Mamá,* I already told you, I'm not going to put *papá* anywhere. It's no trouble for me, just the opposite. . . ."

"Well, that's your choice, just don't come running to me later when you get sick or when Perla wants to leave home. . . ."

"*Mamá. ¡Por favor!*"

"*Sí, m'hijita*, like I told you, I don't want to interfere with your decisions, but I think having your *papá* in your house is causing you a lot of problems, and really, I don't know why you insist so on defending him! Look how life has turned out! The daughter he never wanted to be born is the one who is defending him so much now. . . ."

"Why do you say that, *mamá?*"

"Because that's how it was. For your information, your *papá* wanted me to have an abortion when I got pregnant with you. . . ."

I surrender. There is no way to leave my mother's house unscathed. She always manages to hit me with something that takes me by surprise, that hurts me. I don't know if what my mother has just said is true. If it is, my father must have had his reasons. What does it matter to me now?! She's not going to be able to use that to convince me that my father doesn't love me. There hasn't been a single moment in my life when I ever felt he didn't love me. And now that I think about it, if I were a man and if I had married my mother, maybe I wouldn't have wanted to have children with her either. At any rate, I'm not about to play her game, no, I'm going to chart my own course.

"By the way, speaking of *papá*, he asked me to tell you that he wanted to talk to you. . . ."

"*Mira, m'hijita*, I've told you a thousand times, I don't have anything to talk to him about. I left all that behind a long time ago."

"Yes, I guess you did the same with this photograph."

"Where did you get this?"

"Lolita gave it to me. Who were you pregnant with in this photo, *mamá?*"

"She went to see your father?"

"Yes, but you haven't answered me. Who were you expecting?"

"You, of course, who do you think? Just look how many of these people are dead now! Juanito, Lalo, and Quique are already dead. . . . I think Pepito is too . . . but let's stop talking about these people you don't even know. Tell me, how is Federico, has he put on any more weight?"

"No, *mamá*, he's as skinny as ever, but tell me, why didn't you ever tell me that you and *papá* had had another baby?"

"Did your father tell you about him?"

"No."

"Hmmm! Then was it that nosy Lolita? She's such a gossip, and she was always in love with your father. She'll say anything to cause trouble, that must be why she gave you this photograph. How interesting that she should choose precisely this one!"

"Why would this photo cause trouble? What's wrong with it?"

"Look, Ambar, that's exactly why you and I always end up arguing. You're just like your father, always putting words in other people's mouths, always trying to guess what one is thinking. . . . I don't have anything to hide, and if I did, well, it would be my own business. Children don't have to know everything about their parents, there's no need for that. Look, tell me, would you like it if your children interrogated you about why you got divorced? Have you told them all of your reasons? No, right? Then who are you to come to my house and judge me?!"

"Nobody is judging you, *mamá*. I'm just asking you . . ."

"Well, you have no right! That's all I needed! Who do you think you are to come here to cross-examine me?! What gives you the moral authority to judge me?"

"I already told you I didn't come to judge you."

"Well, that's not what it seems like, *chiquita*, and you'd better change that tone of voice. I am still your mother and you have to respect me! What is done is done! I have my reasons for everything I have done in my life. I don't owe you any explanations. Who said you were my confessor? No one, you hear me, no one. If you are so curious about other people's lives, why don't you go and question your daughter! Ask her how many kisses her *novio* gave her yesterday, or where he touches her! I'd love to hear what she tells you! One has to respect the rights of others!

"Well, since you are so interested in knowing if I had another child, I'll tell you. Yes, I did. And he died. And if you want to know how he died, ask your *papá*. . . . Are you happy now? Why didn't you just ask me, instead of putting me on the spot like this? Why don't you just go now, Ambar, because you've made me mad, and I don't want to say anything that might hurt you. I have never, listen to me, never done anything with the intention of hurting you. I think I have been a good mother to you. I have given you my love, my care, my best. If I have made mistakes, they haven't been serious ones. You should have had a bad mother, then you would have had something to really complain about. A mother who beat you up, or a drunk, or a murderer . . ."

I HAD HEARD ALL I wanted to hear. Curiously, I wasn't surprised. Somehow I already knew. What I can't help noticing is how my mother, whether she's happy or angry, can never say my real name. They say it was my father who chose it, and it seems beautiful to me. He has always called me by my name, Lluvia, except when he sometimes lovingly calls me by the nickname Chipi-chipi, the word for a light kind of rain. But my mother chose to call me Ambar, which according to her is just the same, although to tell the truth, I don't see the slightest connection. My mother says she doesn't like to say the word *lluvia* because it reminds her of the time she and my father spent in Huichapan, when they were newlyweds and it rained all the time. . . . Oh, I just realized something interesting. When Reyes was teaching us Morse code, he gave us a basic lesson in the principles of electricity so we would better understand how the telegraph functioned. He explained very simply how electricity is the flow generated by friction between two different bodies, and about the materials that conduct electricity, and those that ground it. Water is a conductor, so *lluvia*, which means rain, is a conductor, but that doesn't help me to communicate with my mother, because she won't say the word! She always calls me Ambar, which means amber, a grounding material. Though mysteriously, my mother's words, instead of grounding me by their friction, can sometimes produce electric shocks in my brain.

I must find the material that can truly ground her words, because otherwise I can never leave her house unharmed. But now I really need to get back to my father. By contrast, his words are pure alchemy to me. They have the prodigious quality of transforming darkness into light: just like electricity.

Chapter 8

I S IT RAINING, *m'hijita?*"

"Ha, ha. No, *papi*. I'm just hanging the photograph that Lolita brought you."

"¡*Ay, chiquita!* How can you think that I would confuse hammering with the sound of rain? Now all I need to lose is my hearing. . . ."

Lluvia looked out the window and saw that it was in fact beginning to rain, but it was only a few drops, and they were falling silently.

"It *is* raining . . . how did you know?"

"Because I saw the raindrops."

Lluvia laughed at her father's words—she knew he was blind.

"No, really, how did you know?"

"It's simple, I heard them."

"You heard them? Wow! There's no way I could hear that. Maybe a gentle rain, but these little drops, never!"

"That's because you don't try. If you really try, you'll see that little by little you can hear more things. I started with the sounds of my own body, then those of my house, then those of my neighborhood, and so on, until I could hear the stars."

"Oh, right!"

"Seriously, Lluvia. I'm not joking."

"Let's see. Tell me what the North Star is saying right now."

"Right now?"

"Yes."

"Ah, well, I can't, because the noise of your hammering is interfering with our communication."

Lluvia and her father burst out laughing at the same time. She found it was getting more satisfying every day to communicate with her father through the telegraph. She had reached the point of mastering it so well that she no longer needed to use the computer to help her understand her father's messages.

"But to show you I'm not lying to you, let's do an experiment. Think of a question, and concentrate on the star as if it could really hear you. You will immediately receive the answer to your question. If you can't hear anything, I'll tell you the answer myself."

"Any question I want?"

"*Sí.*"

"I don't think I need to ask the North Star who my mother was expecting in this photograph, you could probably tell me yourself."

"In what photograph?"

"The one I'm hanging on the wall."

"It must be Ramiro, your brother."

"His name was Ramiro? What happened to him? Why didn't anyone ever mention him?"

"We didn't?"

JÚBILO ARRIVED HOME JUST in time to hear his brother-in-law Juan announce that Lucha had given birth to a boy. Juan, the doctor in the family, had taken responsibility for delivering the baby. It had been a somewhat complicated labor, but fortunately everything turned out fine. Júbilo entered the bedroom and lay down next to his wife to kiss her hand. Lucha turned her head away from him. She was very angry with him and didn't want to look at him. It was four in the morning and Júbilo had only just returned home, and in an embarrassing state at that. When Raúl was born, Júbilo hadn't left Lucha's side for a minute, but this time she had had to go through labor alone. Well, it's true her mother and brother had been there, but that wasn't the same. Júbilo begged her forgiveness, but Lucha's only reply was a couple of tears rolling down her cheeks. What bothered her most was that her family knew that Júbilo had been out carousing. She had been so careful not to let them know the kind of life she and Júbilo had been living lately. What she hadn't been able to hide from them was the fact that Júbilo had been fired. That had become public knowledge. But Lucha herself had kept her job at the Telegraph Office, ostensibly thanks to the references she had used to get the position in the first place, but deep down she knew perfectly well the reason why don Pedro really wanted to keep her on as his secretary.

Alone in the office, Lucha felt defenseless and vulnerable. But that didn't mean she wanted to quit. She saw no need for it. There were only a few more weeks to go before she could take maternity leave and then she could stay home for three months, being paid her salary while enjoying her time at home with her children and Júbilo. They could then figure out the best way to work out their finances. She was willing to make that sacrifice for her family, and she hoped Júbilo would understand and support her. But that's not the way it turned out.

Júbilo's first impulse after the fight with don Pedro was for Lucha and him to hand in their resignations at the same time, but since Lucha refused, he felt he had no other choice than to stay in his job, to support her, take care of her, and protect her from don Pedro. But it wasn't long before he was fired.

These last few months had been hell for Júbilo. His unfair dismissal had made him very angry. It had been an abuse of power. He was deeply hurt. Great damage had been done. He understood Lucha's wanting to keep her job a few more weeks before her maternity leave, but the situation was very hard for him to bear. His male pride was hurt by his wife's continuing to work . . . and to work with a sick man like don Pedro! He couldn't stop thinking about them being together. He was tormented by jealousy. He felt robbed, stripped of what he treasured most.

As if someone had torn out a lung or sliced off his ears. No, it felt like he had been whipped until his skin was raw, or as if his brain had been filled with dry ice. He couldn't sleep, couldn't eat, couldn't think, everything bothered him, everything upset him. It was as if he had a flaming blowtorch inside him that constantly burned his skin from within. It didn't let him rest for a second. His mind was like a scratched record, playing over and over again in his mind an image that he just couldn't forget: don Pedro caressing Lucha's belly. That son of a bitch! He had dared to touch what was most sacred to Júbilo! He had put his dirty hands on Júbilo's wife. HIS WIFE.

He had profaned Júbilo's temple, his goddess, the love of his life. He knew perfectly well that Lucha was innocent, but he couldn't help being upset with her anyway. He couldn't understand how she could so blithely continue to go in to the office. He was furious with Lucha, with don Pedro, with the whole world, but he made an enormous effort to prevent his family from noticing it. He tried to act just as loving and happy as always, but everyone could tell he wasn't the same deep down, that instead of laughing, he was crying inside.

The first few days after he lost his job, when Lucha had gone to work and Raúl to school, Júbilo would get back in bed, where he could still feel his beloved wife's warmth and smell her scent. To keep from going crazy he would try to think of anything but don Pedro. He tried to listen to *Los Cancioneros del Sur*, his favorite radio program on XEW, but he couldn't concentrate. Music, which had given him so much pleasure, now just disturbed him by reminding him of a Júbilo who had once dreamed of being a singer. So he preferred to turn off the radio and distract himself with other activities. Without Lucha and Raúl, the house grew silent and lonely. Júbilo would slowly wander through it, then go out to buy the newspaper at the stand on the corner, returning to sit down in the *sala* to read it. Even though the *sala* was on the opposite side of the house from the dining room, Júbilo could clearly hear the sound of the dining room clock from where he sat. Its ticktock flooded the house. Júbilo couldn't help listening to every minute going by, imagining what was happening at that moment at the office. Every fifteen minutes the clock chimed a different melody and on the hour it struck loudly. As the clock struck nine, ten, or twelve, Júbilo could imagine the routine at the Telegraph Office with little effort. He knew precisely at what time Lucha would go to the bathroom, when Chucho would read the newspaper, when Reyes would get up for a cup of coffee, or when Lolita would powder her nose. The worst was when he began to think about what don Pedro was doing. His mind would immediately swell with the very thoughts he was trying to avoid, and his torment would begin all over again.

He would imagine don Pedro opening the door to his office and asking Lucha to come in for dictation. He would envision the way Lucha would rise from her seat, carrying her pregnant belly in front of her, and the lascivious look don Pedro would cast at her hips. Finally Júbilo would imagine don Pedro's twisted smile as he closed the door, and there was no way that he, Júbilo, could stop that man from so far away. Not being able to see or hear Lucha drove Júbilo crazy, and his impotence filled him with rage. Life couldn't have imposed a greater punishment on him than to have stuck him in a chair. He couldn't do anything. He was just a spectator. And worst of all, his jealousy prevented him from seeing reality clearly. A translucent gauze, like those used in shadow theater, hung in front of his eyes, distorting his vision and causing him to see enormous, terrifying, invincible monsters and phantoms. When all the time it was just the light on the other side of the screen that turned the shadow of an ordinary hand into a crocodile. Júbilo couldn't envision the day he would be able to take his place in the sun again. Or rid himself of his jealousy. Or bring *la luz*, the light, back into his life.

¡La luz! His Luz María. Júbilo's relationship with Lucha had changed his life in the same way that electricity had transformed the lives of all mankind.

The discovery of how to convert night into day was one of the greatest achievements of the century. It led to a series of appliances powered by electricity that would transform the way of life for city dwellers. The arrival of the radio brought new relatives into every Mexican family. For example, the Chi family was comprised of Júbilo, Lucha, Raúl, and singers Agustín Lara and Guty Cárdenas. When there was no electricity, the family disintegrated, and only Júbilo, Lucha, and Raúl remained. But when his wife and son were also absent, Júbilo felt even worse. The silence and loneliness were unbearable.

But even being left alone wasn't the hardest thing for him to bear, nor that Lucha was continuing to work with don Pedro instead of showing her solidarity for her husband. What was most intolerable for him was that she did so pretending that nothing had happened, as if don Pedro had never caressed her breast, as if in response to such audacity Júbilo had never punched him, as if in punishing the blow don Pedro had never fired him and that now, unimpeded, he could dedicate himself full-time to offending her with his leering. It seemed reprehensible to him that Lucha was stubbornly pretending that things were normal. It turned her into an accomplice, an accessory to a crime.

Júbilo was distressed to see how his wife and all his telegraph operator friends kept quiet, putting up with all kinds of injustices just to keep their jobs. Was there really no other way of earning a living without losing one's dignity? Couldn't they see that without his money and his position don Pedro was a nobody? Hadn't they seen him roll down the stairs like a fat bundle? Júbilo couldn't understand their need to contort themselves, to crouch in fear, to resign themselves to being terrified by a corrupt and despicable man. Oh, how he missed his grandmother in moments like these! Doña Itzel had always had a clear and analytical mind and had been a tireless fighter for social justice. If she were alive now, surely she would already be organizing a revolt in the office to put everyone in his proper place.

Júbilo asked himself what doña Itzel would say if she knew how the progress she had so feared had insinuated itself into the very heart of every home. That there was a radio and a telephone in nearly every house now. That television had just been granted a patent and that people were ready to kill to acquire one of those devices that would allow them to see images broadcast from afar. Besides having proof that her fears had been justified and that progress was not as harmless as had been initially believed, his grandmother would have realized the danger of allowing the owner of a radio station to decide what its listeners should hear and the owner of a television station what its viewers should see. That this control of communication would lend itself to a self-interested management of information and, subsequently, of public opinion. Not that Júbilo was trying to pass himself off as a saint. After all, he had spent his life modifying messages, but he had done so with the sole intent of improving relationships between people. There were many people, on the other hand, who had dedicated their time and energy to linking populations that had previously been isolated from one another, with a clear economic purpose, believing that everything had a value and could be manipulated, exploited, corrupted, commercialized.

Júbilo could easily imagine what his grandmother

would say. She would remove the cigarette from her mouth and speak frankly.

"What's the matter with you, Júbilo? How can you let a man like that, who doesn't care one bit about communication, stay in charge of the Telegraph Office? I die, and everything goes to hell! How can it be that we fought a revolution to give you a better Mexico and now we rot underground while these opportunists benefit from our struggles? Why do you put up with this? Don't you have any balls? How can you let a man like don Pedro, without any morals or scruples, be near Lucha while you're lamenting your fate on a park bench? Don't be an asshole! Get up and do something!"

But what could he do? Force Lucha to quit? First of all, she wasn't a child who could just be told what to do, and, second, under the current circumstances he had no means to support her. If only he had studied to be a lawyer or a doctor like his brothers-in-law instead of a telegraph operator, he wouldn't be in this sad position. He felt like a failure. And to make matters worse, with the arrival of radio communication, the outlook for telegraph operators was rapidly growing bleaker. It wasn't so easy to find a new job. He was dying to get Lucha out of there, but he couldn't imagine how, or when. For the time being he had to accept that they needed Lucha's income, which made him feel even more useless. Fortunately, he still had his night job at the Compañía Mexicana de Aviación and that helped somewhat to alleviate his feeling of failure. Otherwise, he would be slitting his wrists.

Was there a place for him? Was a position waiting for him? Was this part of a cosmic design? In his beloved old neighborhood, everything was related in accordance with a natural, sacred order. The faithful went to church at the same time. The clock at the Museo de Geología chimed the hour punctually. The *bolillos*, those delicious little rolls, came out of the oven of La Rosa bakery at seven every morning and at one in the afternoon, rain or shine. Dr. Atl took his regular walk. Housewives poured buckets of water on the sidewalks and swept them meticulously before their children left for school. The knife sharpener parked his bicycle on the same corner at the same time. Everyone followed a preestablished routine. Júbilo wondered how far one could go in breaking that order. How much could that routine be disrupted? How much was a simple mortal like him allowed to change the rhythm of events? Was his destiny already decided? Could he change it? The only things Júbilo knew how to do were communicate with people, and love Lucha. He didn't know how to do anything else, nor did he want to. As a child he had decided that what pleased him most in life was helping improve people's emotional states and their personal relationships. And, all modesty aside, he thought he did it very well. He was good at communicating, and at loving Lucha. From the first day he had set eyes on her, all he had wanted was to stay at her side forever and to have her be the last person he saw before he died.

That was his desire. However, it seemed the forces of production, industry, and technology were in frank disagreement with his plans.

For the second time in his life, he felt disoriented, frustrated, and disconnected. And, coincidentally, don Pedro was somehow involved in his life again. Júbilo was so furious with him that if don Pedro were standing there in front of him, he would beat him until he wore himself out; he would kick him in the balls until they were rendered useless; he would throw boiling oil into his eyes so he could never again dare to leer at his wife or any other woman. And his hands! Those hands that had had the audacity to touch Lucha, those hands that had robbed poor peasants, that had killed innocent people, that had signed his letter of dismissal. How he would love to lacerate those hands with tiny paper cuts and then pour lime and chile juice on them, so he wouldn't even be able to pleasure himself. Surely that pig don Pedro was masturbating at that very moment, thinking about Lucha's breasts. Júbilo knew for certain that when don Pedro had brushed against her breasts, he had been dying to caress them, to free them from her brassiere and to touch them with his mouth. How could Júbilo not know that!

The day Lucha had taken his hand in her parents' *sala* and put it on her breast as an open invitation to caress her, he had almost died of a heart attack. The first time is always an unforgettable experience, and it was still very alive in Júbilo's memory, but the softness and firmness of her adolescent breast was no match for their roundness and volume now that she was pregnant. Each day he caressed her with greater pleasure. He considered himself so fortunate to have discovered love in Lucha's arms. With her, he had learned how to kiss, to caress, to lick, to penetrate. Together they had discovered the best ways to give each other pleasure. For Júbilo, his hand was his most important sexual organ. With his hand he could give and receive pleasure on a grand scale. With his penis he was limited to caressing the inside of Lucha's vagina, but with his hand he could caress Lucha's entire body. Júbilo had carefully mapped out his wife's erogenous zones. He knew exactly where and how to slide his fingers and the palm of his hand. He had cataloged her points of greatest sensitivity, among which her breasts figured predominantly. Júbilo knew which of her nipples was the more sensitive, how to caress it without causing pain, how long he could suck on it and bite it without injuring her delicate skin.

All of a sudden, he felt a blow to his head. A ball had fallen from the sky and startled him. The laughter of a few small children playing in the park interrupted his musing. Smiling, Júbilo returned the ball to them. Suddenly he felt guilty about sitting in the park at that hour instead of working, and then even more so about thinking of Lucha's nipples in front of these innocent children. He tried to concentrate for a moment on the crossword puzzle he'd been working on, in order to look as if he were doing something, instead of gazing at his navel. Because people are usually judged by what they do and valued by how much they earn, he didn't want anyone to think he was a bum. Now, from any point of view, he felt like a nobody.

A dirty man tottered over and sat down on the bench next to Júbilo, forcing him to stop what he was doing. It was Chueco López. He was terribly hungover. It took him a while to recognize Júbilo, but when he did, he embraced him and cried on his shoulder. He called him his "soul brother" and invited him for a drink at the cantina. Júbilo wasn't too excited about spending time with Chueco, but since he had nothing better to do, he accepted the invitation. It was obvious that Chueco López didn't have any money, so it was Júbilo who ended up paying for the drinks, but he didn't care one bit, because he discovered that the alcohol anesthetized him wonderfully. For a good while he didn't feel any pain at all. He laughed as he hadn't for days. He forgot all about Lucha and her nipples, don Pedro and his greedy hands, the fact that he was semi-unemployed.

Suffice it to say that Júbilo became a devoted client of the bar from that day on. After a few drinks he saw life differently. He could tell jokes, be funny, raise a laugh out of the rest of the drunks.

Júbilo's life rapidly changed. He stopped obsessively looking for work. He felt useful in the cantina. He quickly became the confidant of several drunks and knew he had found the ideal place to spend his mornings. After taking Raúl to school, he would immediately head for the bar. There, he always found someone to play dominoes with, to exchange jokes with, to toast women with. He started smoking more, up to three packs a day now. He would leave the cantina when he heard the clock at the Museo de Geología strike the hour, to pick up his son from school. He would take him to his grandparents' house, and from there he would take the bus to the airport and arrive in time for his job as a radio telegraph operator. He would arrive smelling of alcohol and cigarettes, in a foul mood. When he finished his shift, he would return home and get into bed with Lucha. Hugging her body and with his hand on her pregnant belly, where he could feel the beating of his future child's heart, everything made sense.

Little by little his routine began to vary. It began when, instead of waking up, showering, and getting ready to go to the cantina, he decided he preferred to stay in bed. Then he decided he didn't want to shave anymore. Until the day he decided he didn't want to go to work at the Compañía Mexicana de Aviación.

Any modern psychoanalyst would have diagnosed a severe depression, but since Lucha wasn't one, she exploded. She couldn't put up with any more. All this time she had been pretending that nothing was wrong, but everything was wrong! She had to go to the office every day and fend off don Pedro's flirting firmly but kindly, so as not to anger him. She had to put up with the stench of alcohol emanating from Júbilo's body, even though it made her nauseous just to be near him. She had to eat, even though she wasn't hungry, because she was carrying a child inside her. A child who hadn't done any wrong. A child that Lucha prayed to God would be born healthy and spared from having felt don Pedro's hand caressing it. She had to swallow all of these intimate thoughts. She had to come home tired from work to make the bed, wash the dishes, cook dinner for Raúl, and play with him for a while before he went to bed. She had to hold back the urge to chastise Júbilo for not helping her with the housework, because she knew what a difficult time he was going through. But she couldn't put up with it any longer! If Júbilo thought it was easy for her to keep her mouth shut, he was wrong. It was unbearable to keep quiet in the face of such unfairness. The growing distance between her and her husband was unbearable. She missed making love like they used to do, but now they couldn't even do it at all. She was about to give birth. And on top of all that, now Júbilo didn't want to go to work. How convenient!

They argued for a long time, during which Lucha released all of her anger, which was so powerful that it was much more helpful than a session of psychoanalysis. The next day, Júbilo did go back to work, but not before going to the cantina first to drink himself to the gills. Lucha, completely exasperated, realized she could no longer count on Júbilo, that she was on her own. Fortunately, her long-awaited maternity leave finally arrived. Lucha said good-bye to her job and as soon as she did, the problems between Júbilo and her diminished considerably.

Júbilo's anguish vanished when he could see, hear, and touch his wife. With Lucha's presence in the house, everything went back to normal. Of course, Júbilo preferred to be with her instead of at the cantina. He had a wonderful time with his wife. They went to the market together, cooked together, took baths together, picked up Raúl together, and ate together as a family before Júbilo left for his shift at the airport. Suddenly, his dismissal from the Telegraph Office was converted into something positive. Thanks to Júbilo's having his mornings free, Lucha and he were able to enjoy a relationship worthy of *novios*. That's not to say they were lovers, because Lucha's bulky stomach was in no condition for that sort of activity, but their relationship was filled with more love than ever. They felt reunited and were very happy, in spite of the fact that Júbilo had still not found a new day job.

Júbilo almost managed to forget about don Pedro. His name wasn't mentioned in the house. Maybe that's why Júbilo became so angry the day a telephone call brought him back into their lives. Júbilo had gone out to buy tortillas and was on his way to the kitchen with them. As he passed the bedroom, he saw Lucha sitting on the bed, talking on the telephone. She was tense. Not to appear indiscreet, Júbilo walked on, but kept an ear on the conversation, as much as his hearing allowed. Júbilo finished setting the table while Raúl washed his hands, and when Lucha appeared in the dining room, he knew it was don Pedro who had called. There had been something in his wife's tone of voice that told him. Feigning nonchalance, he asked:

"Who was that?"

"Don Pedro."

"What did he want?"

"Nothing. He just wanted to know how I was, and if we had decided who was going to be the baby's godfather."

"And what did you tell him? He doesn't think *he's* going to be the baby's godfather?"

"It looks as if he does . . ."

"I hope you told him he can't be the baby's godfather."

"I didn't say it directly. I told him we hadn't decided, that we were thinking about it and that I had to talk to you about it first."

"This is ridiculous! I never imagined that he was such a son of a bitch. How can he even think of such a thing?!"

"Calm down, *mi amor.* Raúl will hear you."

"Let him hear me! Lucha, why didn't you just tell him no? Do you really want him to be our baby's *compadre?!*"

"Of course not! I don't want him near my baby at all, but I don't want to be rude to him either. . . ."

"No, of course not! The gentleman deserves all our respect!"

"It's not that, Júbilo, but I don't see the point of antagonizing him, after all he is my boss, isn't he? I have to go back to working with him in a few months and I want to be able to do that in peace."

"You don't have to rub it in, that you're the only one working in this house!"

"Who's rubbing it in? Don't exaggerate!"

"What's the matter, *mamá?*"

Raúl's worried face kept his parents from arguing further, but even he couldn't prevent Júbilo from leaving the house after dinner and failing to return until four o'clock in the morning, after the new baby had been born.

❧

THE NEW MEMBER OF the Chi family was as beautiful as he was shrill. He cried night and day, and soon proved to be the greatest challenge Júbilo had ever faced in his life. Júbilo could usually interpret any child's cry with unbelievable accuracy, but he was totally unable to do so with his own son's. Although he had great difficulty in deciphering Ramiro's needs, he was without a doubt the only one who could calm the new member of the family. With Raúl everything had been much easier. Júbilo never had a doubt whether his older son was hungry or needed his diaper changed. But with Ramiro it was impossible for him to tell the difference. It was harder for him to understand his son's cries than to decode a telegram in Russian. To get even an inkling of what Ramiro needed, they had to bear his cries for over thirty minutes. That may not seem like such a long time, but anyone who has heard a baby crying at full volume knows what we are talking about here.

The baby was driving Lucha crazy, so she was full of appreciation for Júbilo's devotion and dedication to his son's care. At first, she believed he was doing it as a way of redeeming himself and obtaining her forgiveness for not having been with her during her labor, but she soon understood that her husband's interest in the baby was sincere, as was his desire to establish the same kind of relationship he enjoyed with Raúl. Júbilo sang to the child, held him, rocked him with genuine love, but most of the time the infant just cried tirelessly. Ramiro had arrived in this world without an instruction manual, and so Júbilo had to rely on his instincts and follow in the footsteps of his ancestors as a parent. To help him work out what to do and what not to do with the new baby, Júbilo was guided by the ancient practice of trial and error. While he was in the process of figuring it out, the Chi family began to dance to the rhythm of Ramiro's song. The baby set the beat for the entire household. When Ramiro slept, everyone else took advantage of the opportunity to rest for a while, and when he woke, everyone had to get up. There was no way they could continue to sleep. The decibel level of his cries was unbearable and alarming, even provoking complaints from the neighbors. They came to ask whether the baby was eating well enough, or whether he was ill.

But no, the child appeared to be very healthy. He seemed to have no problem seeing or hearing. The sounds he made (you don't say!?), his movements, and his reflexes all corresponded perfectly with the development of a child his age. He urinated and defecated abundantly. There was nothing to indicate a physical imbalance. His problem lay elsewhere and not even Júbilo could understand what it was.

Finally, after studying his son's response to different stimuli, a light went on, and Júbilo realized that his son was bothered by the smell of alcohol. This happy revelation emerged one Sunday afternoon when his brother-in-law Juan had come to visit. Júbilo was holding Ramiro. The child was completely content until Júbilo decided to join Juan in a toast with a glass of tequila, when suddenly Ramiro became infuriated, gesticulating wildly and trembling as if attacked by a monster. As if the infant knew alcohol was the reason behind his father's failure to welcome him into the world, or feared it would separate them. Once this great discovery had been made, that the baby didn't like the smell of alcohol, Júbilo stopped drinking completely and family life returned to normal for a time. Ramiro began to smile and was a delight to the family. These months went by so happily for everyone that when it was time for Lucha to return to work, they all resented it terribly. Fortunately, Júbilo was still working, semi-employed, so Lucha could go to work with confidence, knowing that her husband was at home taking care of Ramiro. In the afternoon, when it was time for Júbilo to leave for the airport, both Raúl and Ramiro would be dropped off at Lucha's parents' house until she picked them up on her way home from work. This new routine allowed the family to enjoy a period of peace.

Until the day a tragic incident was to transform their lives even more than Ramiro's birth had.

JÚBILO'S WORK FOR THE Compañía Mexicana de Aviación consisted of establishing communication with pilots via radio transmitters to give them weather information and instructions for taking off and landing, and, in turn, to receive information from the pilots about their flight paths.

One day, Júbilo was speaking with one of the pilots, with whom he had developed a close friendship, when the connection began to falter. The airplane had just taken off, and Júbilo attempted to reestablish contact with the pilot, but he was unable to. Shortly thereafter, the aircraft crashed and the pilot and many of the passengers were killed. Júbilo was devastated by the tragedy. He felt guilty even though he knew he wasn't at fault. Sunspots had been responsible for the tragedy.

WHEN HE ARRIVED HOME that night, he found Lucha fast asleep. Although he was dying to talk to her about his terrible experience, he felt bad about waking her. He couldn't sleep at all that night. The next morning he didn't get a chance to talk to Lucha either. His wife had to bathe, get dressed, breast-feed Ramiro, and give Raúl his breakfast. Júbilo needed to change his younger son's diaper and soak the soiled one in a bucket, then wash the breakfast dishes. As hard as they both tried, they couldn't find a moment to themselves. But when Lucha and Raúl had left and Ramiro was asleep, Júbilo had time to think about what had happened the previous night, and he became depressed. He called in sick. He couldn't work in this condition. He needed to talk to someone, to unburden himself, but before he went to the cantina he wanted to wait a few hours, to ask one of his sisters-in-law to take care of the children that evening so that he could pick his wife up at work and take her out to dinner. His sister-in-law Leticia wasn't at all surprised by the request. She knew it was Lucha's birthday, and it seemed natural that Júbilo would want to celebrate it with his wife.

Lucha's fellow office workers also knew it was her birthday, but they pretended not to remember so they could give her a surprise party at the end of the day. Don Pedro found his own way to honor her birthday. Early that morning he called Lucha into his office to ask her a special favor. He needed to purchase a gift for a special lady and since Lucha had always distinguished herself with her good taste in clothes, she was the perfect person to advise him. He asked her to accompany him during her break to the Palacio al Hierro to select the most appropriate present. It didn't take Lucha very long to choose a silk scarf. It was far and away the finest and most elegant they had. Don Pedro asked the salesgirl to wrap it. The whole process didn't take very long. They quickly headed back to the office and along the way, as they were about to cross the street, don Pedro took Lucha's arm. At that very instant Júbilo was turning the corner and so he happened to see the couple laughing and looking carefree. Don Pedro was carrying a wrapped gift adorned with a large red bow.

INSTEAD OF FOLLOWING THEM into the Telegraph Office, Júbilo decided to turn around and calm down by walking a little. He didn't want to make a scene in front of his friends. But it didn't help, because when he arrived minutes later to pick up his wife, he found her trying on a scarf and saw the box he had just seen don Pedro carrying lying open on Lucha's desk. His soul filled with rage. Feigning a calm he didn't feel, Júbilo asked Lucha who had given her the scarf and she, so as not to anger him, said that it had been Lolita. She didn't see any reason to tell him it was a gift from don Pedro, much less to remind Júbilo that it was her birthday, since he hadn't remembered, or at least he hadn't congratulated her yet.

It was true that Júbilo had completely forgotten about her birthday. Between his insomnia the night before and his feelings of guilt, of course he hadn't remembered! On the other hand, even if he had been aware of it, all he would have done was to buy her some flowers rather than an expensive gift. He wasn't in the habit of demonstrating his love that way. But don Pedro was, and Lucha, who was so accustomed to receiving gifts on her birthday, couldn't help feeling pleased when don Pedro had given her the gift she had unwittingly helped to select.

For Júbilo, this was the first sign that don Pedro had resumed wooing his wife, but what worried him most was that, this time, it seemed to please her. If not, then why was she trying to hide from him the fact that don Pedro had given her the scarf?

What Júbilo wasn't able to see was that his wife's happiness was due to his own arrival in the office rather than to receiving the scarf. Júbilo's apparatus for receiving messages seemed to be damaged. His mind confused the codes. It mixed up the clues he received from the outside world and converted them into an indecipherable tangle. Usually Júbilo's mind was very sharp, and he always understood why people said "I hate you" instead of "I love you" and vice versa. But now he kept misinterpreting the messages Lucha sent him. To Júbilo, his wife was like the Enigma machine used by the Germans during World War II to send encoded messages.

During the war, the radio served as an essential strategic tool. It was used to send orders to the troops on the front lines, but the signals were easily intercepted by the enemy. All they needed was a radio tuned to the same frequency. The German army, in accordance with its rigid routines, sent out orders at the same time each day, and the Allies took advantage of this to intercept the signals and listen to their orders. To foil the Allies, the Germans invented a cryptographic machine, which changed one letter of the alphabet for another. One could use this modified typewriter to write normally, but as each letter was printed, it was substituted by another letter, with the aid of twenty-six cylinders containing thousands of combinations. The only way to decipher an encrypted message without knowing the relevant code was by guessing the position of the rotors at the beginning of the message, which was practically impossible.

But thanks to the collaboration of a number of notable mathematicians, the Allies soon developed an apparatus similar to the German Enigma, making it possible to decode the German messages. However, it was difficult and demanding work. At first they had to be laboriously guided by the number of repetitions of each particular letter, but then the Fish machine was invented, a teletype that coded and decoded messages much more swiftly. This process, which required so many hours of work, wasn't wasted. After the war ended, it served to help advance the development of the computer.

Júbilo's mind too was a sophisticated cryptographic machine, only it was out of order at the moment and was therefore making errors in interpreting signals. His wife's delight was because she was happy to see him, not because she had received a scarf as a gift. The difference was very significant, but he couldn't read it correctly. For the third time in his life, this had to do with active sunspots interfering with radio communication systems. Júbilo was suffering the catastrophic consequences of this phenomenon, in both his personal and his professional life. Luckily, Lucha's reaction to her husband's surprise visit was so enthusiastic that it overcame his jealousy. She covered him with kisses and hugged him, and used their closeness to remedy her husband's faulty memory.

"I knew you hadn't forgotten my birthday."

Júbilo realized his oversight immediately. How could he have forgotten something like that?! Since Lucha was thirteen years old they had always celebrated her birthday together, so although he was in no mood for celebration, he made an effort to put aside his jealousy and his problems to fete his wife as she deserved. He took her to dinner at Café Tacuba, and the meal turned out to be a powerful aphrodisiac. Café Tacuba was an integral part of their sentimental history. Among other things, Júbilo had asked Lucha to marry him there, and it was there that she had announced that he was going to be a father for a second time. Sitting at their regular table and being waited on by their usual waiter had a relaxing effect on Júbilo, and this helped him to recover his usual good mood. During dinner he was able to tell Lucha about his terrible experience the previous night, and he received from her all the support and understanding he expected and needed. As he held Lucha's hand, light flooded his brain and illuminated the darkest corners of his soul. Gradually, the loving energy between them began to build up, and they hurried through the rest of their dinner so they could go home, eager to give themselves up to the pleasures of love. Júbilo's birthday present to Lucha was the best night of lovemaking that she'd ever had in her life and that she would ever have. It was a magical night. They made love as they never had before. But from then on, events were fated to overtake them, events that would hurl them from heaven down to hell, with extraordinary speed.

Lucha and Júbilo woke up aching but full of energy, despite having hardly slept all night. Lucha quickly dressed for work. She was careful, as always, to choose the least suggestive dress, in the hope that this would protect her most from her boss's indiscreet glances. She gave her husband a long kiss on the mouth and hurried off to work. Júbilo took charge of Raúl and Ramiro.

Júbilo had now been awake for two full days and nights, one because of the airplane accident and the other because of their lovemaking. But the previous night had filled him with sufficient energy to overcome his exhaustion. He functioned much better at work than usual. His batteries were so highly charged that he didn't feel tired again until he opened the door of his home late that night. He expected to find Lucha at home, but, surprisingly, she wasn't there. Instead, he found his mother-in-law, who tried to explain as best she could that Lucha had called her from the office to tell her that she couldn't pick up the children: she had asked her mother to take them home, and to explain to her husband that she would be home late, because there was an emergency at the office.

This seemed very strange to Júbilo. As hard as he tried to imagine what kind of "emergency" could occur in a telegraph office, he couldn't think of any. He thanked his mother-in-law for looking after his children, and he swiftly took charge himself. After putting the children to bed, he lay down and turned on the radio. *La Hora Azul* had already started. Agustín Lara's voice filled the bedroom.

> Sun of my life
> Light of my eyes
> Feel how my hands caress your smooth skin
> My poor hands, broken wings
> Crucified beneath your feet . . .

It didn't take long for the image of Lucha lying crucified on their bed to appear in his mind's eye. Júbilo imagined her as she had been the previous night: burning, passionate, madly in love. It excited him to remember Lucha's look of total ecstatic abandonment. What a woman he had!

Where could she be now? Why hadn't she called? He was really worried. Soon the telephone rang. It was Júbilo's mother-in-law. She was worried too. Her daughter had never done anything like this before. To calm her, Júbilo told her that Lucha had already come home and was breast-feeding Ramiro. With those words he was not only sincerely trying to ease his *suegra's* worry, but also trying to prevent her from calling again, because the ringing of the telephone made him even more nervous than he already was. He tried to listen to his radio program to clear his mind of negative thoughts and closed his eyes to concentrate even more.

> *Tell me your roses bloomed for me*
> *Give me the smile that gives me hope*
> *Tell me I haven't lost you*
> *Give me the tranquillity of your soul*
> *Come, with the moon I will show you my cabaña*
> *Counting the hours of the night, I will wait*
> *Know woman that my love for you is true*
> *Know it, know it well . . .*

He couldn't stop thinking about Lucha. The music only served to remind him of the previous night, because these same songs had provided a musical background for their lovemaking. Lucha! Was she thinking of him too? Try as he could not to imagine anything bad, he failed. It seemed very suspicious that she hadn't been in touch. The only reason he could think of was that she'd been in an accident . . . or that don Pedro had invited her out with him. His nerves were on edge. To calm them he turned first to cigarettes and then, when they ran out, he moved on to alcohol. It was bad luck that just at that moment Ramiro woke up. It was time for him to eat, but his mother wasn't there to feed him. Júbilo tried to give him a bottle filled with cow's milk from the refrigerator. While it was warming up, he held the infant in his arms so that his crying wouldn't wake Raúl. But as soon as Ramiro noticed the smell coming from his father's body, his crying escalated dramatically, and there was no way to quiet him.

Júbilo had to apply cologne, brush his teeth, suck on mints, and coo to his son for hours before he was able to make him fall asleep again. He put Ramiro in his crib and lay back down on the bed. The alcohol and accumulated exhaustion of two full days and nights without sleep took effect and Júbilo slept deeply for a few minutes. It wasn't long, but it was long enough for Ramiro to wake up again, pull the blanket that his father had covered him with over his face, and suffocate.

Júbilo awoke to Lucha's screams. She had just arrived home, and before lying down to sleep beside her husband, she had leaned over to kiss her baby, only to find he was dead. Through his confusion and Lucha's hysterical sobbing, Júbilo managed to ask:

"What happened?"

"Ramiro is dead!"

Júbilo just couldn't understand what was happening. He approached his wife, who was pounding her fists on the wall, and tried to hold her arms so she wouldn't injure herself. At first, Lucha let her husband hold her, but when she smelled alcohol on him, poorly disguised by the cologne, she pushed him away brusquely.

"Are you drunk? Is that why you didn't hear the baby?"

Lucha now aimed her fury at Júbilo and struck him without mercy. At first Júbilo offered no resistance, he felt he deserved it, and much more. He felt guilty. But then the guilt became so overwhelming that he lashed out at her savagely in return.

"What about you, where were you? Why didn't you hear your baby? Were you out whoring around?"

Lucha stopped crying. She couldn't believe what she had just heard. It wasn't possible that Júbilo had said such a thing to her, much less at a time like this. She moved away from him slowly and walked toward the bathroom. On the way she picked up Raúl who, rubbing his eyes, had come looking for his parents. Lucha closed the bathroom door behind her and locked it. She didn't want to see Júbilo. She couldn't bring herself to explain to him that she had come home late because don Pedro had raped Lolita. That she had taken her friend to the doctor and hadn't left her side until she was able to calm her down a little and take her home. Lucha didn't have the strength to talk. She decided right then and there that she didn't have anything more to say to Júbilo.

THE DEATH OF HIS son was devastating for Júbilo. Failing to hear his own child was the worst thing he had ever done. He who considered himself specially gifted at being able to hear anything, from thunder to absolute silence, just couldn't grasp what had happened. He who had believed that there was no such thing as total silence had simply been deaf to the world for a few minutes. He who knew that no matter how quiet the air was, there were always hearts beating, planets spinning in the heavens, bodies breathing, plants growing; and all producing sounds, but he hadn't heard anything! He hadn't heard anything!

FROM A VERY YOUNG age, Júbilo had realized that not everyone could hear as he did, that there were whispers, buzzes, creaks that were imperceptible for most people, but which to him were penetrating noises. Even the sound of an insect walking was audible to Júbilo. When he was taken to play at the beach, he would say to his grandmother, "Do you hear how the sand sings?" He was referring to the sound that the tiny grains of sand make as they are blown by the wind. To most people, that "song" is only sometimes audible in large sand dunes, but never on a sandy beach. To Júbilo, however, the intonations produced by the sand were quite clear.

Without a doubt, Júbilo had an ear that was adapted for hearing shortwave frequencies that not even modern machines could pick up. That sensitivity had been a problem for him, since over the years the city had become filled with an overpowering noise, like that of a rumbling truck. The sound often bothered him, it filled his ears with whistling sounds that sometimes even gave him a headache. And after all that, what good had it done him? He hadn't heard his own child dying!

"*Papi*, ARE YOU LISTENING . . . ?"

"Maybe he can't hear you."

"Did you give him a sedative?"

"No, I gave him an analgesic, because he complained of a pain in his stomach, then he fell asleep. . . ."

"*Papi*, wake up, *chiquito*. *Mamá* has come to see you. . . ."

Don Júbilo opened his eyes immediately. He couldn't believe his ears. Lucha was there. His heart began to pound and his stomach trembled and started to hurt again. He had been waiting for this moment for so many years.

Lluvia was also taken by surprise. She had repeatedly asked her mother to visit her father but Lucha had stubbornly refused. It was a unique occasion that she had finally appeared at the house, and without notice. Lluvia couldn't remember her parents speaking to each other since the day she was married, thirty years earlier. For as long as she had been able to reason, she remembered the distance between her parents, they even slept in separate bedrooms. Once, Lluvia had asked her father why they hadn't divorced. He replied that in those days a man was never granted custody of the children and that he wouldn't have been able to bear being separated from them. To Lluvia this didn't sound like sufficient reason, but she hadn't insisted. Although it seemed odd, she had an inkling that her parents had maintained their strange relationship because of a loving force hidden beneath their apparent distance that continued to draw them together. Whatever the reason, she was thankful for the opportunity she'd had to enjoy her father's presence at home while she was growing up, although to strangers her parents' relationship had been a total mystery.

It was at her wedding that her parents had seen each other for the last time, and now it was in her house that they saw one another again, and Lluvia could only bless the occasion. As soon as she had explained to her mother how her father "spoke" via the computer, Lluvia said to them:

"Well, I think you two have a lot to talk about."

To which her mother replied:

"Yes, that's right."

Before closing the door, Lluvia managed to hear her mother say to her father:

"I hate hating you, Júbilo."

Chapter 9

LUCHA ARRIVED A LITTLE late for work, but happier than ever and unaware that it was the last day of complete happiness she would ever have. From that day forward everything would change, but at that hour of the morning nothing seemed wrong. No, more than that, in Lucha's eyes the world shone even more brightly than usual and glowed warmly with a pinkish hue. She was totally in love with her husband even though they'd been married for ten years. She had never imagined that was possible. Much less that she would still be learning new ways of making love. Júbilo had turned out to be a wonderful sexual partner.

The previous night they had discovered new positions that didn't even appear in the *Kama Sutra*. And through them she had experienced incredible multiple orgasms. A night like that was well worth ten years of financial hardship. None of the little problems Júbilo and Lucha had gone through in their marriage was able to diminish in any way their love for each other. Even Júbilo's recent inclination to drink didn't seem like an insurmountable obstacle. Lucha was fully aware it was temporary and that Júbilo relied on it only as a way to forget about his problems, since for a man like him it must be very difficult not to be able to support his family. Sometimes Lucha even felt guilty about being so demanding. She only hoped that it was clear to Júbilo she wasn't interested in money itself, but only in its power to help her provide her family with a decent life.

She wasn't the only one who was concerned. Lolita had told Lucha on several occasions that perhaps she was asking too much of Júbilo and criticized her for having so many aspirations. Lucha didn't take this the wrong way. She knew Lolita had said what she did out of love, that she was guided by her honesty and integrity. Lolita was a patient woman who didn't expect anything from life. She was always the first to get to the office and the last one to leave. She performed her work quietly. She never acted in an irresponsible or unconventional manner. She was discreet, prudent, timid, modest, and very, very proper. She was so eager to please others that she never made a comment that was out of place: she was driven by an overwhelming fear that people would stop liking her. When she was a young girl, her father had abandoned her and her mother, and she never wanted to be abandoned again. So to avoid it, she was ready to do anything for anybody, to the point of servility. However, her need to please only caused men to run away from her. She never had a *novio* and she always fell in love with men who couldn't love her back.

Lucha loved and respected Lolita very much even though she knew her friend was in love with Júbilo. Lucha didn't hold this against her. After all, Júbilo was the kindest and most loving person in the world. When the three of them were still working together, Lucha had always been pleased to see the looks Lolita threw at her husband from time to time. It never bothered her, just the opposite, it made her feel proud. Nor did she take it the wrong way when her dear friend defended Júbilo with sword drawn, or that Lolita seemed to be so worried about the situation Lucha and Júbilo found themselves in.

Lucha considered Lolita her confidante and she was grateful for her sincere concern. The only thing Lolita didn't seem to understand was Lucha's attitude toward money. Lucha had received a very specific education from her parents about money and how to use it. She knew very well what money could buy and she didn't hesitate to spend it. That didn't mean she was a compulsive spender. She simply knew that money, among other things, was important for a sense of security. To feel one could live peacefully in a house that could withstand earthquakes, rain, and the cold. Her great preoccupation about having money to pay for a good school for her children stemmed from her belief that the better their education, the better they would be able to provide for their own families. That's why she had felt so vulnerable during the first months of her marriage to Júbilo. It was the first time she had been exposed to hardship, and it terrified her.

Fortunately, it hadn't taken her long to realize that she

would never find a more worthy man than Júbilo, and that the way to stop worrying about money was to go out to work herself and help her husband support them. And since she had started working things had improved greatly. She felt that her marriage was more solid than ever and that Júbilo's emotional state would improve as soon as he found another job. And she was willing to help him all she could to make sure every centavo they earned was used properly.

Because of this, whenever Lucha bought anything, she liked it to be the best, and also the best value. She was of the firm belief that you get what you pay for. And she was very particular about the way things looked too. She believed that living in a clean, pleasant, harmonious environment raised the spirits. Lucha had a rare talent for spotting the best buys the moment she entered a shop. They never escaped her notice even when they were hidden among many other things. She always found the most beautiful dress, which unfortunately usually turned out to be the most expensive. But Lucha never wasted much time in hunting down bargains. According to her reasoning, it was much better to always buy the best, because cheaper things usually faded or shrank the first time they were washed.

When she went into a furniture store, it was the same. She was always drawn to the most expensive piece of furniture made with the highest-quality wood and the best finishes. She knew from experience that they would last the longest, just as she knew that the best drink was the least harmful to one's body. She had the same good eye for evaluating people. From the first moment she saw Júbilo she had appreciated his other virtues as much as his physical beauty. He was an intelligent, sensible man, possessed of a wonderful sense of humor, sensitive in his dealings with others, passionate in bed, respectful, gentlemanly, in short, truly unique.

Lucha was amused by Júbilo's jealousy toward don Pedro. She could *never* have even looked at a person of such low social, spiritual, and physical standards. Don Pedro was the complete opposite of the light, harmony, and good taste radiated by Júbilo. Don Pedro was a swarthy, ugly, evil-looking, disgusting, disrespectful, immoral, vulgar opportunist, who didn't know what proper manners were, much less how to treat women and show them respect. She wasn't about to trade down. And don Pedro was out of his mind if he thought he could buy her with a stupid scarf. Lucha wasn't crazy enough to renounce Júbilo and her children for such an unworthy man. He was just a poor fool with money in his pocket. If money had been the only thing that mattered to her, she could have gotten it ages ago, and by the handful, from her boss. But that wasn't what she wanted. She wanted much more than that. She wanted to spend the rest of her days by Júbilo's side and to remain just as much in love with him as she was now, as she had been last night! She blushed as she remembered again what Júbilo and she had done in bed.

Her employer's presence in front of her desk brought her back to reality. Don Pedro was offended because

Lucha had left the office the previous evening without even saying good-bye to him, even though she had been wearing the expensive scarf he had given her! What hurt him most was seeing the look of love she gave her husband. He had never inspired that kind of look on anyone's face, much less a woman like Lucha, and he was determined to do whatever it took to make that woman his: and to amortize the cost of the scarf. Women were all equally ungrateful, they only wanted men for their money, but he was going to teach them how to treat a man like him with respect. Tired of being brushed off by Lucha, he wasn't willing to wait any longer to get his hands on her. He was full of rage and planned to overcome her resistance to him any way he could. The cold, distant tone Lucha used in her dealings with him was extremely irritating. He had tried everything, but nothing worked with her. He had to change his strategy to persuade her to sleep with him. He had invested a lot of money in Lucha and now he intended to collect for all the flowers, the chocolates, and that damned scarf. He was fed up with feeling ignored and disdained.

He had decided to punish her by doing the same to her, but she hadn't even noticed. And to make matters worse, the ingrate had allowed herself the luxury of arriving late for work! So he had punished her by loading her down with a ton of dictation. Almost everyone had left for the day and the office was practically deserted.

"Have you finished?"

"Almost."

"*Ay*, Luchita! You left so quickly yesterday, you didn't even say good-bye to me. I was planning to invite you to dinner."

"I appreciate the gesture, but you know I'm married. I went out to celebrate with my husband."

"I hope he treated you well."

"Yes, he did."

"Did he give you a present?"

"The best."

"Better than the scarf I gave you?"

"You know what, don Pedro? Your question is in very poor taste. I suggest you don't ever ask me a question like that again, well, that is, if you ever want to get anywhere in society."

"You really think you're some fine filly, don't you?"

"Yes, I do."

Don Pedro felt the sudden urge to slap Lucha to wipe the look of disdain and superiority with which she stared back at him off her face. And Lucha felt the sudden urge to hand him her resignation right then and there. She didn't like the way she was being treated one bit. No, señor! Her family's financial situation was still dire, but she wasn't pregnant anymore and she could easily find another job, even a better-paying one, where she wouldn't have to put up with a cretin like don Pedro. But neither of them immediately acted on their impulses. Don Pedro swallowed his aggression, turned around, and entered his office, shouting from the open doorway:

"Lolita, please come to my office!"

Instead of finishing the letters in front of her, Lucha began to write her letter of resignation. She had already made up her mind, but she was going to do it properly, not impulsively. That's what education and intelligence were all about. When she had finished the document, she placed it in her desk drawer, picked up her purse, and left the office. Before going home, she wanted to get Júbilo some bread from Café Tacuba to prolong the good taste left in their mouths from the night before. As she walked back to her car, she suddenly realized she had left the car keys on her desk. She turned around and returned to the office. She couldn't help smiling like an adolescent in love—she loved this feeling of distraction.

When she returned to the office, there was no one there. The desks were empty and silence reigned. Lucha's footsteps echoed through the building. But the light was still on in don Pedro's office. Lucha tiptoed past so her boss wouldn't hear her. She didn't want to be caught alone with him. As she noiselessly picked up her keys with her fingertips, Lucha heard the sound of sobbing coming from don Pedro's office. She froze for a few seconds to make sure she had heard correctly; yes, there it was again, a woman was crying.

Lucha steeled herself as she opened the door: she saw Lolita lying curled up in a corner, weeping. Lucha ran to her side and with horror deduced what had happened. Lolita's clothing was torn, and her stockings were blood-stained. She was in a state of total shock. When she saw

Lucha, she clung to her friend and began to scream desperately. She told Lucha that don Pedro had raped her. Then she begged her not to tell anyone, because she would die of shame if anyone else knew, especially Júbilo. Lucha consoled Lolita as best she could and tried to convince her to file charges against don Pedro at the police station, but Lolita stubbornly refused. She didn't think she could bear the humiliation. So Lucha tried to persuade her to go to the hospital, but again met with resistance. Finally, after a long time, Lucha was able to convince Lolita to come with her to her brother Juan's house. He was a doctor and would attend to her. Lolita accepted on the condition that Lucha stay by her side the whole time.

Lucha kept her promise and stayed with Lolita, holding her hand and wiping her tears, until she could finally take her home and put her to bed. They had to break the news to Lolita's mother: her daughter had been the victim of a terrible attack and that was why she had arrived home so late and in this condition.

Lucha was dead tired when she got home. Seeing Lolita in such a sad state had been a very jarring experience. She never imagined that something even more terrible was waiting for her. Ramiro's death represented the end of all that she held dear in life: her family and her love for Júbilo.

That night, don Pedro had not only robbed her friend of her virginity but at the same time profaned her own home. He had destroyed Lucha's image of Júbilo and Júbilo's image of her. How could Júbilo have doubted her?! Lucha had thought that if anyone in the world knew her best, it was Júbilo. If she had ever put all her faith, her trust, her dreams, her intimate desires in someone, it was him. And suddenly she realized that the seventeen years they had known each other meant nothing. With a single question, Júbilo had ended it all. How could he have called her a whore? Didn't he know her? What good had it done to give him not only her body but her very soul? It seemed unbelievable that the person she trusted most, and who supposedly loved her more than anyone else, was the same person who had now destroyed her whole world, a world she had never dreamed could deteriorate or be devalued. It was unbearable to find out that the one man she thought was different from all the rest turned out to be just like them. Lucha decided she would never again allow him, or any other man, to hurt her. She wanted to have nothing more to do with men.

The day after Ramiro's funeral she asked Júbilo for a divorce. Because of the emotional state they found themselves in, Júbilo asked that she wait a few days for a decision, but Lucha didn't want to listen to him or to accept any of his arguments. Her heart had been destroyed; she had buried it beside Ramiro. She felt as if she had been murdered. Just like don Pedro.

That same day, a headline had appeared on the front page of the newspaper: MURDERED WITH THE SAME WEAPON THAT KILLED HIS FORMER LOVER. It was an account of don Pedro's death at the hands of an unknown woman. The story read:

His was a life of cockfights and women. The director of the Telegraph Office was found dead this morning outside a hotel in the Plaza de Garibaldi, in the company of one of his regular girlfriends. He was killed by a .44 caliber bullet from the same gun with which he had killed another young mistress years ago. After that incident, due to his money and influence, he escaped prosecution. Pedro Ramírez emerged from obscurity during the Cristero Rebellion amid rumors of arms dealing to go on to enjoy an enviable political career. Ramírez held several administrative posts in the national government, among which the most important was as federal representative for the state of Puebla. According to initial investigations, Pedro Ramírez left his office on Friday evening and joined several friends at El Colorín, an infamous nightspot located in the Plaza de Garibaldi. At his hip was the .44 revolver, the same weapon responsible for his death later that night. Waiters at the club stated that Ramírez was a regular customer who often frequented the place in the company of a variety of women. Official reports indicate that later that night, Pedro Ramírez left the nightclub and walked toward a nearby hotel in the company of two young women with whom he apparently intended to spend the night. A short distance from the nightclub, the group was met by a third woman, who argued loudly with Ramírez and, during the ensuing scuffle, Ramírez's weapon discharged and he was killed. The mystery woman fled the crime scene, and no physical description of her is available.

Apparently she had never been seen in the area before, and the only information police were able to gather was that she was well dressed, which leaves many questions still to be resolved in this homicide investigation.

WHEN A CHILD DIES so many questions remain unanswered, particularly when the parents are burdened with feelings of guilt. What would have happened if I hadn't fallen asleep? Could I have saved the baby if I had been at home? Would my son still be alive if I hadn't been drinking? Does God punish? What have I done to deserve this punishment? Am I really capable of protecting and caring for my family? How can this kind of neglect ever be forgiven? How can I ever overcome this sense of betrayal? They each had their own doubts about themselves, but it was clear that neither Lucha nor Júbilo was able to trust their partner again. The tragedy put an end to that. They could no longer even look each other in the eye. The pain of their son's death was unbearable, and each with their mere presence reminded the other of it.

Some people believe one should forgive as easily as one loves, but others refuse to accept this because they just can't forget. Júbilo couldn't forget that he had been in charge of the child when he died, nor that a well-dressed woman had killed don Pedro in a jealous rage on that very same night. Lucha couldn't forget that Ramiro had died because of Júbilo's neglect, much less that that neglect had been caused by his drinking. To forgive it is necessary to accept what cannot be changed, and neither of them was able to do that, because their own guilt prevented it. Lucha felt that if she hadn't been so demanding, Júbilo would never have felt so useless and wouldn't have started drinking. Ramiro had died because Júbilo had fallen asleep, but if she had been at home she would have heard him. Júbilo thought that if he had been capable of earning enough money, Lucha would never have felt the need to go out to work. She would never have had to deal with don Pedro and fall into his clutches, as he suspected. Only the passing of years could heal their souls, and then they still had to clear up any lingering doubts. It would take them both fifty-two years, an Aztec solar cycle, to talk about what happened that night and to finally put their minds at rest.

But at the time, neither of them could see clearly; they were both busy trying to forgive the unforgivable, to find a little relief, to free themselves of guilt, to somehow continue living with the terrible memory of what had happened. So the news of Lucha's new pregnancy took them by complete surprise and raised new questions. They were in the middle of divorce proceedings. Júbilo felt this was not the right time to have another child, but Lucha felt just the opposite. To her, the unborn child represented a connection between them. She saw it as a living testimony of the love they had shared, as proof that all those years had been worth the trouble, and she would fight tooth and nail to keep it. But Lucha had decided the child would belong to her alone. She didn't want to share it with Júbilo. She struggled to get the divorce through as quickly as possible, even though it was against the advice of her entire family. All she could think about was kissing and cuddling her unborn child, the product of the most loving night of her life, the night before Ramiro's death. She felt with this new pregnancy life was giving her back something that it had mercilessly taken from her. That was how she wanted to see it. And looking at it more closely, she even thought she should be grateful to the gods for the help they were giving her. To begin with, they had removed don Pedro from her path so her life could be improved. After all, the wretch more than deserved to die. But what Lucha just couldn't fathom was why they had taken Ramiro from her. That was something she would never understand, even though they seemed to be trying to console her with the arrival of a new child.

FOR JÚBILO, IT WASN'T so easy to accept becoming a father for a third time. He was worn out, empty, he didn't feel up to facing a new child, to saying: "I am your father. I brought you into this world and I am the one who is supposed to provide you with food and clothing, but guess what, I don't have any money. And I'm supposed to take care of you and love you, but let me tell you, I'm no good at those things: I tend to get drunk and fall asleep while my children suffocate. I don't think I'm good for you; I can't watch out for you while you sleep; I'm no good at that, I might let you die."

At the moment, Júbilo didn't even feel capable of taking care of himself. He was filled with self-recrimination. The fear of hurting others made him look for ways to efface himself as a human being, to avoid everybody else, to numb his conscience. It hurt to wake up. It hurt to see Raúl. It hurt to look at Lucha. It hurt to smell the flowers in the garden. It hurt to walk. It hurt to breathe. The only thing he wanted to do was die. To get rid of his physical body once and for all, because emotionally he was already dead. So he chose to hang out in the cantina, to stay there all the time. To end his pain. To end his struggle.

There, he could forget about everything and everyone. The only effort he had to make was to raise the bottle to his lips. He would spend all day drinking and at night he would lie in the cantina's doorway begging for money for more drink, without washing, without eating. His inseparable companion during this time was Chueco López. Chueco was his teacher in his new life on the street. When the cantina was open, they used its bathroom when they needed to, but when it was closed, to relieve themselves they had to go to the Sagrada Familia church, the same church where Lucha and Júbilo had been married years before. It was sad for everyone in the neighborhood to see Júbilo in this condition, and no one hesitated to give him money when he asked for it. Besides the affection in which he was held, everybody owed him a favor, so they couldn't refuse, even though they knew that Júbilo would use the coins they gave him to keep on drinking. Everyone knew his child had died and they understood his despair. Some tried to talk to him, to give him advice, but Júbilo couldn't hear them; he was lost in the alcohol. His physical and mental condition deteriorated rapidly. He suffered all kinds of calamities. He was robbed, and his jacket and shoes were stolen, but he didn't even notice. Some days he woke up vomiting, others, soiling himself, still others, thrashing and striking the ground. His legs became swollen, his feet cracked and split open, and his heart bled day and night.

And that's how he lived until he had completed a cycle of fifty-two days. The number fifty-two was, of course, significant to the Aztecs, because the sum of its digits yields seven. Seven times seven fits inside a year, so to them fifty-two represented a complete cycle of life.

The fifty-two days that Júbilo spent drinking represented a phase he had to go through to realize he didn't really want to die. He came to this conclusion one day when his brother-in-law Juan came looking for him. Júbilo could no longer stand up. When he saw Juan, he clung to his hand and said, "Help me, *compadre!*" Juan took him to the hospital, where Júbilo began his recuperation.

We're talking about a slow and painful convalescence that included learning how to live again. The first thing Júbilo had to face was the withdrawal from alcohol, then regaining movement in his legs and arms, and finally the proper functioning of his whole body. But the most difficult thing without a doubt was trying to win back his family. When he left the hospital, Lucha was already seven months pregnant. She had gotten herself a new job at the National Lottery, in addition to her original job at the Telegraph Office. Because don Pedro was dead, she had not found it necessary to hand in her resignation after all. She was more beautiful than ever, but she didn't want to have anything to do with Júbilo. She was pleased enough that he had recovered, she had even been the one who told her brother Juan where to find Júbilo, because she had heard it from a neighbor. She had followed his recovery with great interest from a distance, but that's how she wanted to keep him, far away from her and her children.

Júbilo had to make an enormous effort to get back on his feet, to find work again, and to convince his wife he was going to fight to preserve his marriage any way he could. Lucha's parents played an important role at this stage. Although they had once tried to dissuade their daughter from marrying Júbilo, they now did everything they could to convince her she should forgive him and allow him to return home, because they loved him like a son. They had had years to see what a wonderful man he was, and his mother-in-law had become his best ally. She never tired of defending him, and she didn't stop praising him until she managed to soften Lucha's heart and convince her daughter to meet with the man who was still her husband. They had never finalized the divorce, because the law prohibited it while Lucha was pregnant.

Júbilo arrived at the house looking very presentable. His in-laws had taken Raúl home with them so Lucha and Júbilo could speak openly without interruption. As soon as they saw each other, their bodies felt the urge to run toward each other and embrace, but their minds restrained them. Júbilo was thin, but he reminded Lucha of the boy she had first seen when she was thirteen. Lucha was more voluptuous than ever. Her enormous belly drove Júbilo crazy with desire. After talking and crying for a long time, Júbilo asked her to show him her stomach. Lucha lifted her maternity dress so Júbilo could admire her ripeness, and they ended up in bed, holding each other tightly.

A heavy rain fell from the sky and filled the room with the smell of damp earth. Lying there holding Lucha and listening to the rain, Júbilo distinctly felt his soul return to his body. The rain was a reminder that he had been dead, that months before, his spirit had migrated to a higher sphere, and that it had now returned to occupy its rightful place back on Earth. The rain represented the resurrection of water, droplets that had evaporated from the earth to take on a new form in heaven, and then return to Earth once more. The sound of the rain falling and the thought of the child in Lucha's womb were for Júbilo the best song of life ever. It became clear to him that he was being given a second chance to live, and he knew he couldn't waste it.

The love Lucha and he shared had generated a new

existence, palpable inside this belly on the verge of bearing fruit. And the beating heart of that being was the best reason for remaining like this, in a close embrace, for the greater part of the afternoon, until they were interrupted by the onset of premature labor. Soon a seventh-month newborn arrived into the world like a gift from heaven.

Júbilo called her Lluvia and swore he would never, ever be separated from her, no matter what. He wanted to be all ears to keep her safe, and he was ready to give her all the love he had inside him. He was eager to show his appreciation of each extra day of life he had been given. And so he did. Júbilo remained living under the same roof as Lucha until Lluvia got married.

Those years weren't all sweetness and light. Lucha and Júbilo were never able to completely patch up their marriage. Don Pedro had left behind him a great shadow that loomed over everything, from their house to the office. Júbilo got his job back at the Telegraph Office, but it wasn't the same anymore. Something bad had happened there, and Lucha had kept it a secret.

"WHY DIDN'T YOU TELL me this before? Why did you keep it to yourself for so long?"

The sound of the telegraph transmitter's ceaseless tapping filled the room. Júbilo moved his fingers swiftly, but he received no answer. His blindness prevented him from realizing that it had grown dark and that Lucha couldn't read the computer screen anymore to see what he was "saying."

Then Lucha stood up from her chair and ran to the bedroom door. Opening it, she shouted at the top of her voice:

"Ambar! Please come here!"

Lluvia came running, alarmed by her mother's shouts and thinking that her father's condition had taken a turn for the worse, but when she entered the room she saw what the emergency was, and immediately set about rectifying the situation.

"What is your father saying?"

"He says . . . it was his duty to take care of you and to fill your life with laughter, and he couldn't do it . . . he asks you to forgive him for having failed you. His only aim was to love you. He understands he didn't always know how, but you have always been, and will always be, the person he has loved most."

That isn't what don Júbilo had signaled at all, but he loved hearing his daughter interpret his words in that way. He made a sign of complicity and gave a deep sigh. Finally Lluvia had dared to give voice to what she desired more than anything. Lluvia understood this. And she knew that she hadn't made it up; she was convinced that she was simply repeating the words she had heard so long ago, while she was waiting in her mother's womb for the best moment to be born. When Lluvia had interpreted her father's words she had merely been faithful to the voice that had echoed through the corners of their house for so long without ever daring to make itself heard.

When Lluvia saw that her mother's eyes had taken on an unusual shine, she knew her interpretation had been right. She had managed to unearth emotions that had remained buried beneath pride and aloofness for such a long time. Lluvia was about to discover a new side to her mother. At first, she had been surprised by the look of pain on her mother's face when she first saw how sick Júbilo was. She had never imagined her mother could feel so much on his behalf. And now as her mother's eyes glistened with love, Lluvia felt as if she had made a discovery much more important than that made by the archaeologist who found Coyolxauhqui. All these years, beneath layer upon layer of coldness, her mother had kept hidden a loving gaze that could melt anyone's heart! The shine in her eyes came from the deepest recesses of her heart. It was unbelievable that it could have gone unnoticed. Lluvia had assumed that her parents hadn't communicated at all for a long time, but now she became aware of her error.

She reflected on how in 1842 Samuel Morse had discovered that cables weren't necessary for transmitting messages and that wireless telegraph communication was possible, since electric currents traveled just as swiftly without cables as with them. He made that discovery one day when he saw a boat on a river accidentally cutting through an underwater cable: he realized that this didn't interrupt the message that was in the process of being transmitted.

Similarly, as Lluvia witnessed the way her mother's hand rested on her father's without a word passing between them, it proved to her that inside the resonating matrix that makes up the cosmos, the transmission of energy occurs on a permanent basis. She wondered whether this invisible and intangible communication had always existed between her parents, and whether she was only just realizing it now that she had discovered she had a wonderful facility for perceiving it.

Curiously, don Júbilo's illness, which brought so much suffering with it, was what allowed Lluvia to discover that her parents' bond had been unbroken since her birth. She would love to have known this when she was younger. What serenity it would have brought her childhood to realize that although communication between her parents seemed to be broken down, in fact energy continued to circulate from one to the other. Even though the lines were down, their love kept traveling as swift as their desire! She only needed to look at her parents' intertwined hands to understand so many things. Her mother's rage, her constant frustration at not being able to kiss and embrace her husband as she wanted, the way she directed her anger at her children instead of at him. Her father's yearning, the way he sought out music and turned it into a substitute for Lucha's caresses. In a second it all made sense to her. How she would have liked to understand much earlier, but everything happens in its own time and there is no way to speed things up to one's liking. For example, it took don Júbilo his whole life to rebuild the bridge that had been broken. He finally managed it a mere moment before dying, and he left the world in peace.

He spent most of his final day in a coma, unable to use his telegraph transmitter. He had waited for Lucha to visit him before he died. Lluvia was convinced that the light in her mother's eyes would illuminate her father's way in his travels beyond this world. They said good-bye without speaking, but with much love.

THERE IS NOTHING LIKE popular wisdom. There are so many sayings that ring so tremendously true, and yet their full meaning isn't really felt until one experiences them firsthand. I have often repeated the saying "You never know what you've got till it's gone," but it wasn't until my father died that I understood what these words really meant. His absence is immeasurable. There is no way to explain it, to quantify how alone I now feel. The only thing that is clear to me is that I am not the same anymore. I will never again be don Júbilo's daughter. I will never again feel like a protected child. I will never again know the reassurance that there is a man in this world who will always give me his unconditional support, no matter what.

It is difficult for me to conceive of a world without my *papá*. He was always by my side, in good times and bad. When I was sick, my *papá* was there. When I was upset, my *papá* was there. During celebrations and holidays, my *papá* was there. During school vacations, my *papá* was there. Always smiling, always attentive, always ready to help me, whether it was to take my children to school, to crack walnuts for *chiles en nogada*, or to accompany me to the flea market at Lagunilla. Whatever it was, from the moment he opened his eyes until he shut them for the last time, my *papá* was always there for me.

I know it's selfish to think this way. The life my *papá* led in his last months was no life at all. He suffered so much. He hated depending on others. His death was really a blessing, and that it happened the way it did. Surrounded by love, with all the people who loved him so much at his side, in his own bed and not in some cold hospital. The only thing that still pains me is that I didn't manage to take him to see his beloved *K'ak'nab* again, the beach at Progreso, where he first learned to swim. We had planned the trip, but he was never well enough to let us make it. At least he was able to say good-bye to the sun. The morning he died, he asked me to put him in front of the open window to greet it one last time. He fell into a coma and that afternoon he died. Following his final instructions, we dressed him in his white linen suit, the one he wore when he danced *danzón* with my *mamá*. And then we brought him to the funeral home.

It was a cloudy afternoon; the sun never made an appearance, but my mother arrived wearing dark glasses. It was obvious she was wearing them to hide her eyes, which were swollen from so much crying. It didn't surprise me at all. I could identify with her pain. What did surprise me was that she called me by my real name. As we began to walk through the cemetery, my mother took me firmly by the arm and said, "Don't let go of me, Lluvia." She seemed so vulnerable and small! I imagined how lonely she must feel to have lost for the second time the man who had been her husband.

When we returned home from the cemetery, after tearful good-byes with Lolita, don Chucho, Nati, and Aurorita, I closed the door to the room that had been my father's and didn't open it again for a week. I couldn't bear to see his empty bed, his silent radio, his still telegraph, his empty chair, all desolate and abandoned. But after seven days had passed, the need to feel my father's presence drew me back into his room and made me sit in his chair. The room still held his scent, and the arms of the upholstered chair still retained his warmth, but he was no longer there. I would never again hear his footsteps, the sound of which had always brought me such peace. From the time I was a little girl, as soon as I heard him come home, I would know everything was going to be all right, that any problem would be lessened just by his presence. Now that was all gone. I thought about the overwhelming experience of watching him die, of being at his side the moment he departed. I had thought I was well prepared for facing his death, but I was wrong. One is never prepared. The mysteries of life and death are too powerful. No mind can fully embrace them. It is very difficult to understand what occurs in the third dimension.

We only know that the deceased are no longer here, that they have gone and left us alone. Anyone who has seen a lifeless body knows what I am talking about.

Seeing my father's stiff body lying on his bed reminded me of the horrible feeling I had experienced one day as a child, when I saw a marionette hanging from a nail, after a puppet show. A few moments earlier I had seen it speak, dance, walk, and suddenly there it was, immobile, empty; it had lost its soul, had stopped being a character and become just a piece of painted wood. The difference between the marionette and my *papá* was that the puppet could come back to life in the hands of the puppet master, but my father couldn't. That body would never again speak, move, laugh, walk. That body was dead, and I now had to sort out his possessions.

I preferred to deal with it right away to avoid prolonging my mourning. I opened his drawers and began to fold his clothes, to organize his records and his books. I set aside his records by Virginia López and Los Panchos for myself. Then I discovered a small box that obviously held his keepsakes. I opened it slowly, out of respect. Inside I found a photograph of my mother when she was about fifteen. An oval picture of me from elementary school. A photo of my children, and one of my brother. A small envelope containing a curl of baby hair and a note in my father's handwriting that said, "memento of my beloved Ramiro." A small notebook with notations of significant Mayan dates, and a detailed drawing of a Mayan stela. A guitar pick and a matchbox. When I opened it, I discovered my first tooth, with a note by my father recording the date it had fallen out.

That day instantly came back to me. My *papá* had taken me to my bed and helped me put the tooth under my pillow for the mouse to come and take away.

"What's going to happen to my tooth, *papá?*" I asked.

"Don't worry, *m'hijita*, the mouse will come and take it away, but in its place he'll leave you some money," he replied.

"I already know that," I insisted, "but later, what's going to happen to my tooth?"

"Later?"

"Yes, once the mouse has it."

"Oh! Well, he's going to keep it in a little box with the rest of his most treasured possessions."

"No, *papi*, you don't understand. I want to know what's going to happen to my tooth. Is it going to fall apart?"

"Well . . . yes, but not for many, many years—it will eventually turn into dust—but don't worry about that now, you just go to sleep, my Chipi-chipi."

MY FATHER WAS RIGHT. The "mouse" kept my tooth with the rest of his most treasured possessions, and although it was still in good condition, it is going to end up turning into dust, but not for many, many years. Maybe I will never see it. But these thoughts helped me to overcome my pain. I stayed there for a while thinking about the dust. "Ashes to ashes, dust to dust." Everything that lives ends up as dust. We walk amid dust from butterfly wings, flowers, stars, rocks. We breathe the dust of fingernails, hair, lungs, hearts. Each minuscule particle of dust carries with it traces of memories, nights of love. And at that moment, dust stopped being a symbol of accumulated solitude for me, and became just the opposite. Millions and millions of presences of beings that have lived on Earth are in that dust. Floating there are the remains of Quetzalcóatl, Buddha, Gandhi, Christ.

In that dust were mingled bits of skin my *papá* had left behind, little pieces of his fingernails, his hair. They were spread over the whole city, over the pueblos he had traveled through with my mother, over my whole house.

Not only that, but my father lived on in my body, in that of my brother, my children, my nieces and nephews. His legacy, both physical and emotional, was present in all of us. In our minds, in our memories, in the way we lived, laughed, spoke, walked. Pondering on this during the funeral, it allowed me to go over and give my brother a heartfelt hug, something I hadn't done in many years. And it allowed me to reconcile myself with life.

With the passing of the days, my life has started to return to normal. At times, as I go about my daily business, I get the feeling that my father is accompanying me, and that fills me with a sense of peace. Sometimes I can even hear his voice echo clearly in my head. I'm not sure if my belief that my *papá* is close by comes from my desire to feel good, but whether it's true or not, I do know that wherever my *papá* is, he would love to know that I have gone back to taking the astronomy classes I gave up when I got married, that I am learning the Mayan language, and that as soon as Federico's son, my grandson, has learned to read and write, the first thing I shall teach him is Mayan numerology, so that his heritage is not forgotten.

Last night I had a very revealing dream. My *papi* and I were riding in his old car, the '56 Chevy. We were driving to Progreso, on the Yucatán peninsula. The highway was full of butterflies. Some of them struck the windshield. I was driving and suddenly my *papi* asked me to let him drive. Without waiting for my reply, he reached for the steering wheel. Despite his blindness, I wasn't afraid to let him drive. My *papá* laughed happily and I joined in. I felt a little afraid only on the curves, because he didn't turn the wheel fast enough. On a sharp turn, to my surprise, he kept going straight ahead; but instead of falling into the void, we flew up into the air. We speeded over several provincial cities and in all of them people on the ground waved at us. Many campesinos eagerly waved their sombreros, as if they recognized us. When we reached the ocean, my *papi* said, "Look, Chipi-chipi," and he quickly jumped in the water and began paddling around. I was surprised, given his Parkinson's, that he could move about so easily.

A sound slowly awakened me from this deep dream and brought me back to reality. It was a message being tapped out in Morse code on the wooden head of my bed, which is turned to face north. Curiously, it came today, on the fourteenth of February. In addition to celebrating love and friendship, in Mexico we also use this day to commemorate telegraph operators, although not many people remember that anymore.

Telegraph operators, those people who played such an important role in the history of telecommunication, have now been forgotten. I can understand why no one would want to remember don Pedro, but it makes me sad that few people would take a moment, before they go on-line on their computers, to remember that in its day the telegraph was as important as the Internet is now, and that telegraph operators made an essential contribution to the enjoyment we have of instant communication today. Well, sometimes life seems ungrateful, but it doesn't really matter. The interesting thing about the communication process is that in one way or another it allows us to express the words that come from within us. Whether they are written, spoken, or sung, they fly through space charged with the echoes of all the other voices that have preceded them. They travel through the air bathed in the saliva from other mouths, humming with the vibrations from other ears, and throbbing with the beat of thousands of hearts. They cling to the very core of our memories and lie there in silence until a new desire reawakens them and recharges them with loving energy. That is one of the qualities of words that moves me most, their capacity for transmitting love. Like water, words are a wonderful conductor of energy. And the most powerful, transforming energy is the energy of love.

All those whose lives my father helped to change would always call him on February fourteenth to honor him. Today, the first ones to call were Jesús and Lupita. They were very saddened by the news of his death, the death of my *papá*, the telegraph operator, the man who knew how to unite thousands of people, who knew how to express their hopes and desires. And ultimately, that is all that really matters, that we all remember him. He will always endure in our memory, thanks to the transforming power of his words. And by the way, the words in the message that was tapped out on my headboard were:

"Dear Chipi-chipi, death does not exist and life is wonderful. Live it to the fullest! I shall love you always. Your *papá*."

ABOUT THE AUTHOR

LAURA ESQUIVEL is the award-winning author of *Like Water for Chocolate*, which has sold over four and a half million copies around the world in thirty-five languages; *The Law of Love;* and, most recently, *Between Two Fires*. She lives in Mexico City.